"I want to give you a warning, Kurt."

Rolt's voice was calm as he moved to his desk, not even bothering to glance at his brother. "You've had a clear field with Alanna for long enough. Now I'm joining the competition."

Gasping, Alanna couldn't believe that she had heard right. Rolt was talking about her as if she wasn't even in the room; referring to her as if she was some prize to be won and not a human being capable of deciding for herself which man she preferred. Hadn't she made it plain she heartily disliked him?

Rolt had made a fiasco of her homecoming. Nothing had gone as she had planned!

JANET DAILEY AMERICANA

GIANT OF MESABI

Harlequin Books

TORONTO • NEW YORK • LONDON
AMSTERDAM • PARIS • SYDNEY • HAMBURG
STOCKHOLM • ATHENS • TOKYO • MILAN
MADRID • WARSAW • BUDAPEST • AUCKLAND

The state flower depicted on the cover of this book is pink and white lady's slipper.

Janet Dailey Americana edition published May 1987
Second printing June 1988
Third printing June 1989
Fourth printing July 1990
Fifth printing September 1991
Sixth printing January 1992

ISBN 0-373-89873-8

Harlequin Presents edition published November 1978

Original hardcover edition published in 1978
by Mills & Boon Limited

GIANT OF MESABI

CHAPTER ONE

THE PLANE'S SHADOW skimmed across the treetops. Within the pine forest, the blue of a Minnesota lake winked briefly in the sunlight. A ribbon of concrete ahead beckoned to the plane's shadow.

Inside, Alanna Powell gazed eagerly out the window, her heart quickening as the airport's terminal building came into view. Tawny blond hair framed the fresh-scrubbed beauty of her face. Her pointed chin had a willful thrust, and the sparkling light in her violet eyes, her most outstanding feature, revealed a flashing spirit. Yet her finely-shaped lips displayed a hint of vulnerability.

There was a slight jar as the plane's wheels touched and rolled on the runway. Alanna pressed her lips together, absently checking the freshness of her lipstick. Futilely she searched the terminal for a glimpse of Kurt, knowing it would only be the sheerest luck if she saw him from here.

A tightness gripped her throat. What if Kurt wasn't there to meet her? With an almost imperceptible movement of her head, Alanna shook away the thought. When she had phoned him yesterday to say she would be on this flight from Minneapolis, he had agreed to meet the plane without hesitation. He hadn't even waited for her explanation that she wanted to surprise her parents.

It was crazy to be so apprehensive, she told herself. But, her mouth twisted wryly, that was what love did to a person. She hadn't seen Kurt since the Easter break almost two months ago. He had made it plain that he was attracted to her then, but so much could have happened since then.

The plane rolled to a stop at its terminus of the Chisholm-Hibbing airport. Unfastening her seat belt, Alanna rose to join the file of passengers disembarking. A fluttering hand moved down from the waistband of her wheat tan skirt. Her fingers unconsciously checked to make sure the buttons down the front were securely fastened, except for the last two above the knee that let the hem flap to reveal her shapely legs and hint at the smoothness of her thigh.

There was no sign of Kurt among the group of people gathered to meet the arriving passengers. A glance at her watch verified that the plane was on schedule. Perhaps he had been delayed. Her steps slowed as she scanned the area.

A familiar male figure was bent over a drinking fountain, and Alanna's heart leaped in joyous relief. All her fears vanished in that instant of recognition.

"Kurt!" She laughed his name, her heels barely touching the floor as she ran to him. "I thought you'd forgotten about me!" As he straightened and turned, she started to fling herself into his arms with uninhibited happiness. A half step away from the broad chest, she realized her mistake. "You!" Anger and astonishment mingled in the accusing pronoun.

Her retreat was cut off by the iron circle of his arms curving around her waist. "Don't stop now," he said, and the faintly cruel line of his mouth twisted into a cynical smile. "If I'm going to stand in for my brother, I might as well receive his kiss, too."

"No!" The strangled denial was wasted breath.

A large hand slid up her spine to twine its fingers in her tawny hair, tugging at the tender roots to force her head back. Her hands strained uselessly against the looming muscular chest while the lower half of her body was crushed against the granite hardness of his.

Alanna couldn't escape the descending mouth or the steel band of his embrace. She had not even time to stiffen in resistance to his invasion as he kissed her with hard, slow pleasure, taking advantage of her momentary paralysis of disbelief.

In the next second, she was released. A pair of blue eyes, a deep shade of indigo, glittered over the vivid flush in her cheeks. A rush of anger flamed within her, the exhilaration of battle flashing through her nerve ends.

"How dare you!" she breathed tightly.

Half-closed eyes surveyed her indignant stand, a thick screen of dark, masculine lashes veiling their expression. A smile without humor curved the mouth that had only seconds ago bruisingly possessed hers.

"Give me your claim tickets and I'll get your luggage. I suggest you wait until we're in the car to unleash your temper and wounded outrage." His gaze flicked around them to indicate the public surroundings.

Her poise was already shaken, and the trace of mockery in his tone didn't do anything to restore it. Indeed, calling attention to their mildly interested audience worsened it. Seething inwardly, Alanna fumbled through her purse for her ailine ticket and the baggage checks attached to it. With rigid control, she thrust the papers into his outstretched hand.

How could she have been so blind not to recognize that it wasn't Kurt but his brother, Rolt Matthews, Alanna railed silently. There were surface similarities between the two. Both were tall and dark with leanly muscled physiques. But only a fool would mistake Rolt for Kurt.

Her gaze fastened in a violent glare on the arrogant set of Rolt's shoulders as he walked away from her. He was taller than Kurt by an inch or two, with a catlike fluidity to his easy strides. His dark brown hair was the shade of coffee, shot with a golden hue in the sunlight, not bordering on brown-black as Kurt's was. It grew long and thick about his collar, brushed carelessly away from his face.

Their facial features were another dissimilarity. The sun-bronzed planes of Rolt's face held a quality of ruthlessness. The carved lines around his mouth were etched with cynicism. Overstamping it all was a rakish air of virility, blatant and overpowering, a dominant force that demanded to be reckoned with.

Rolt Matthews was of the dark world and Kurt was of the day. Handsome and charming, Kurt was the antithesis of his older brother. Alanna had been drawn to him since their first meeting nearly five years ago when she had been fifteen. Yet it was only this Easter that Kurt had taken any notice of her and the attraction she had always felt was able to blossom.

Her lips trembled, tender from the hard mastery of Rolt's kiss. She had never had any time for Rolt Matthews. As surely as she had been drawn to Kurt, she had been repelled by Rolt. Whenever his gaze rested on her, so startlingly blue with its enigmatic glitter, she was uncomfortable. His hooded looks with their trace of mockery disconcerted Alanna more than she cared to admit. Yet Rolt seemed to know it and found amusement in her unease.

That was why he had kissed her, she guessed. Her fingers clenched the clasp of her purse, the metal as hard and unyielding as his chest had been beneath her hands. Her flesh burned where it had been in contact with the male length of him.

During Easter, she had made no secret of her attraction to Kurt. There had been no need, since he returned it. Always when Rolt had been around, which fortunately was seldom, he had watched them with aloof interest, leaving Alanna with the impression that he found their relationship amusing and somehow juvenile.

Juvenile. Alanna breathed in sharply at the word. Heavens, Kurt was twenty-nine, she was twenty-one. They were adults, not a pair of infatuated teenagers as Rolt seemed to regard them. No doubt his five-year advantage caused him to look down on his brother. If the odd bits of gossip were accurate, Rolt's considerably broader and more intimate associations with women probably made him regard their budding romance with a cynical eye.

The approach of firm, purposeful strides aroused Alanna from her inward reflection. Her gaze bounced away from the male figure, effortlessly carrying her heavy luggage. Rolt paused for an instant beside her, his alert gaze sweeping over the profile she presented to him.

"My car is parked in the lot outside," he stated. "Shall we go?"

"The sooner the better," Alanna agreed briskly.

There was a mocking tilt of his head to indicate that she should precede him. The glint in his indigo eyes told her that he knew how much she disliked him and found it amusing. With a haughty sweep of her head, Alanna walked out of the building, only to have to wait for Rolt to point out his car. It was on the tip of her tongue to tell him she would find her own way to her parents.

Yet such an action bordered on cowardice, since it indicated that she might be slightly intimidated by his presence.

Stacking her luggage at the rear of a black Mark V,

Rolt unlocked the passenger door and reached in to push the trunk button before stepping aside. There was no way Alanna could avoid the strong fingers that clasped her elbow and helped her into the car. The instant the door was closed, she rubbed away the hard imprint. When the luggage was safely stowed in the trunk, Rolt slid behind the wheel.

Loath as she was to break the silence, Alanna knew she would not be able to sit quietly until she had learned why Kurt had not met her. Something told her that Rolt was not going to volunteer the information.

Glacing at his aloof profile out of the corner of her eye, she felt a surge of violent emotion rise inside. He was so self-assured and blandly indifferent to everything except his own desires.

"Why wasn't Kurt able to meet me?" she demanded finally.

His gaze flicked briefly to her, masked and unrevealing. He started the motor and reversed the car out of the parking lot. "There was a breakdown of some equipment at the plant and he was unavoidably detained. An emergency."

The answer was too glib. Alanna guessed it was meant to be, but she couldn't keep from rising to the bait. "Obviously it wasn't so great an emergency that you were detained."

There was a movement of his mouth in what should have been a smile, but other than that, Rolt made no verbal acknowledgment of her comment.

His attention remained focused on the road as he pulled into the traffic.

"I don't suppose it occurred to you to handle the emergency in Kurt's place and leave him free to meet me." She compressed her lips tightly, anticipating the answer before he gave it.

"It occurred to me." Again his gaze swung to her for fleeting seconds, lingering suggestively on her glistening lips before returning to the highway. And again there was that mirthless curve of his mouth that was somehow cold and foreboding. "But I would have been denying myself our meeting."

"Why?" Her temper flared at his unnecessary reminder of the kiss he had taken. "It wasn't a pleasant meeting."

"Perhaps not." The wide shoulders lifted in a gesture of unconcern for her reaction. "But it's one that isn't easily forgotten."

"Nor forgiven," Alanna added darkly.

"Do you expect me to apologize?" It was obvious by his tone that he found the thought amusing.

Her fingers curved over the leather arm rest, golden tan to match the upholstery of the seats. She wished it was his hard flesh her nails were digging into instead of the pliant leather.

"Not you," she declared in a contemptuous breath. "I don't think you have any code of ethics."

"Ethics?" A dark eyebrow arched. "What does ethics have to do with a kiss?"

Alanna sputtered for a few seconds, too incensed

by his apparent disregard for the fact that she was his brother's friend and, she hoped, more than that.

"I am dating your brother," she pointed out tightly. "And I don't think it's accepted conduct to go around kissing his girl."

"Are you his girl?" His narrowed gaze pinned her. Knowing she couldn't answer, he negated the need with a cool smile. "Not that it matters whether you are or not. I've always taught my brother to share."

"I have some say in that," Alanna retorted. "And believe me, I have no interest in you—"

"—making love to you," Rolt finished for her, the wolfish slash deepening near his mouth.

"I was about to say 'paying attention to me,'" she snapped, reddening under his bluntness. "But if you want to be more explicit, I'll agree with that, too."

Her sideways look of reproach did not meet his gaze. After she had glanced away, Alanna found herself looking back at the strong hands gripping the wheel of the powerful car. They controlled it with such ease, supplely guiding the car into curves and around corners. She knew those same hands would be just as expert guiding a female form into the intricacies of love. Their touch would be firm and authoritative yet teasing and arousing as they caressed her—

With a guilty start, she stared straight ahead. Her cheeks flamed at the direction her thoughts had taken. She despised the man! How could she possibly even imagine such things? Had she suddenly lost all sense of decency and self-respect?

"Why are you so upset because of one kiss?" His gaze flicked to her heightened color.

Self-consciously she flipped a thick strand of tawny hair over her cheek, smoothing it over her skin to conceal her embarrassment and appear nonchalant.

"Or do I just rub your fur the wrong way?" His low drawling voice seemed to reach out to stroke it right. "Does it bother you that I find you—"

"Amusing?" Alanna filled in the adjective to deprive him of the opportunity to mock her further.

"Is that what you think?" Rolt returned smoothly.

Her chin lifted a fraction. "It's true. That is the way you think of me—something that's amusing, someone you can tease with your cynical humor. Understand this, Rolt, I will not be an object for your amusement. You'll have to find one somewhere else."

"Maybe I don't want to look elsewhere. What then?" he baited.

Alanna stared out the window to avoid his mocking visage, letting her violet gaze study the commercial district of Hibbing. "Don't toy with me, Rolt," she said tautly. "I'm not interested."

"But maybe I'm interested in you." He said it quietly and so seriously that Alanna's curiosity forced her to glance at him. The bronze mask of his features told her nothing, but the lazy glint in his eyes seemed to make light of his statement. "Is it so difficult to believe that I might find you attractive?"

His gaze swept over her figure with disturbing assessment. Its brief hesitation on her legs caused Alanna to draw the buttoned front of her skirt together at the hem. The cruel line of his mouth quirked at her action. He had done it deliberately, knowing the way it would unnerve her. And she hadn't disappointed him. She bit into her lower lip to keep from screaming her frustration and anger.

"It's impossible," she insisted, more because she thought there was a chance it could be true and doubted her own ability to fence with a master of the game.

"Tell me, Alanna—" he slowed the car at a stop signal and gave her his undivided attention as the car idled at the red light "—are you still a virgin?"

She breathed sharply. "That's none of your business!"

"You're going out with my brother," Rolt pointed out. She became even more agitated when she noticed he was watching the uneven rise and fall of her breasts. "I was curious."

"You can keep on being curious!" she flashed.

The light changed to green and he shifted the car into drive, laughing softly in his throat. "I don't have to be. You've already answered my question." There was a sliding blue look, glinting and mocking. "Are you saving yourself for Kurt?"

The heat searing her skin was unbearable. "Well, not for you," Alanna hissed. "Never for you!"

"Careful," he warned with laughter in his voice. "Never is a long time."

Alanna was about to argue that it wasn't long enough as far as Rolt was concerned, but at that moment she realized that, instead of turning at the road that would take her to her parents' house, he had stayed on the highway.

"You missed the turn," she pointed out.

"No, I didn't."

He sounded so certain that Alanna glanced back over her shoulder to the crossroads, nearly convinced that she was mistaken. "My parents live down that road."

"I'm not taking you home."

He wasn't serious! One look at his face told her he was. Her mouth opened, speechless for an instant. "Where—"

"Kurt is at the mine. You did want to see him, didn't you?" he mocked.

"Is that where we're going?" Alanna demanded, tired of his games.

"Of course—" taking his foot off the accelerator "—unless you want to go directly home."

"I would like to see Kurt," she admitted, seething at his deliberate failure to tell her. Sarcasm coated her tongue as she added, "It never occurred to me that you would take me there. After all, Kurt does have an emergency on his hands."

Her gibe rolled off his back like water from a duck. "I think he can be spared for a few minutes to see you. I can take over for him."

"Just as you could have to let him come to the

airport to meet me." Alanna rubbed her fingertips on the throbbing ache in her temple. "The same way you've taken over from my father," she murmured bitterly. "I regret the day he ever sold controlling interest to your company."

"The iron vein had played out. Your father didn't have the financial ability nor the knowledge to switch the operation to processing taconite. If he hadn't sold out to us when he did, in another year he would have been bankrupt. That is the truth, whether he or you will ever admit it," Rolt stated in a cold, unemotional tone. "Besides, you wouldn't have met Kurt—or me."

Alanna didn't comment on his observation. The buildings of the city were no longer rolling past her window. The landscape was mostly rural, pine studded and green. They were on the Taconite Trail Road in the middle of the Mesabi Iron Range.

In this arrowhead area of Northern Minnesota, the major source of the nation's iron ore had once been mined. The veins in the Vermilion, Mesabi and other ranges had been so rich, it was thought in the beginning that they would last for ever, but progress and war had revealed a lack of foresight. Now the abundant taconite was being processed into iron, enormous plants rising above the trees.

Behind the green façade, the story of the passing of the large iron mines was told to those observant enough to read. Abandoned open pits were being fast reclaimed by nature, trees and brush taking over the empty land. The yellow flowers of the hardy bird's foot trefoil plant covered old tailings.

Alanna had spent her childhood here. The twisting, winding canyons and ridges had been gouged out of the earth by heavy machinery to expose the iron veins. With the riches plundered, foliage invaded to inhabit the land again.

Mesabi was an Ojibwa Indian word, meaning Land of the Sleeping Giant. It was a name given to the range of mountains because of its resemblance to the sleeping figure of a man. Virgin forests had once covered its slopes, tramped by fur-trappers, felled by lumbermen's axes or uprooted by iron-seeking escavation equipment. The towering pines the Ojibwa had known, ten feet in diameter and more, were gone, and young trees grew in their place.

While the sleeping giant rested, other giants walked the land. Amethyst and shimmering in resentment, Alanna's gaze slid to the impassive man behind the wheel. That was how her father had once described Rolt Matthews, as a giant, referring to his stature as a man, not to his physical size. He was tall and muscular and a compelling figure, but that was not what set him apart from others. Or so her father had told her.

Dorian Powell, her father, was a sensitive, erudite man. Despite his earnest attempts, he had never been a successful businessman. The iron mine—the family wealth—had been inherited from his father and grandfather. When the vein played out, so did the family resources.

In her heart, Alanna had known Rolt's statement that her father would have been bankrupt if his firm had not purchased controlling interest was accurate. But she also knew her father's reasons for selling were not purely the monetary gain for himself. His main concern had been the economy of the area and the people who worked for him. After the sale, he had stepped aside, relegating himself to a mere stockholder.

When she had protested and insisted that he should have a more active part in the transition and future operation, he had smiled and shook his head.

"It's a job for only one man. It's going to take someone who will drive himself as hard as he does those around him, without concern for personal feelings. When you own a business and have people working for you, there's a tendency to play God. You can't do that and be successful. There were times when I was more concerned about an illness in some employee's family than I was in the day's production. You can't let things like that bother you. You've got to stand apart from the workers, immune to their problems. You can't let personal feelings, yours or anyone else's, interfere with business. It can't matter whether a man likes you or curses you behind your back. A man in charge has to be above that—a giant. You can't let anything stand in your way if you want to be successful. Rolt Matthews is that kind of a man."

"Cold and ruthless is what you mean," Alanna had retorted.

"I suppose you could describe him that way," Dorian Powell had agreed, "but he'll make the company successful and himself in the process. Everyone else will benefit from his success, including ourselves."

Cold and ruthless. The adjectives described him aptly. He kept himself apart and seemingly above others. To Alanna's knowledge, since Rolt had taken over control of the company, he had never associated with anyone from the company outside of business hours. Kurt was the only exception. Even then the occasions they were together were rare.

Her gaze shifted for the second time to the strong, tanned hands on the wheel. She wondered briefly about the women he had known. Alanna didn't doubt that the touch of his hands could bestow pain or joy, but she doubted whether Rolt ever felt anything himself.

The car slowed and turned off the highway, and Alanna glanced up to see the entrance gate to the plant. The security guard posted at the closed gate bent slightly to view the car's occupants. With a respectful nod to Rolt, he swung the gate open and let them through. As they drove by, Alanna thought she recognized the guard. His hair had grayed and his shoulders were stooping with advanced years, but he still looked familiar.

"Isn't that Bob Schmidt?" She had only been out to the plant once in the last five years, then just to pick up her father. "I went to school with his daughter, Justine."

"It could be. I don't know his name."

Rolt's lack of interest in the man's identity was apparent in his indifferent response. Her father would have known. He prided himself on knowing the name of every man who worked for the company. But Alanna did not bring the fact up. She had too recently recalled her father's assessment of the qualities and traits needed to be successful.

It wasn't important that Rolt know the guard's name. As long as the payroll clerk and the computer knew, that was all that mattered to him. His attitude chilled Alanna regardless of its business merits. She admired her father more as a sensitive failure than she did Rolt's success as an unfeeling giant with physical needs and no human emotions. Thank God, Kurt didn't take after his hardhearted brother.

Inside the gates, the plant bustled with activity. Smoke billowed from pollution-controlled stacks atop the large buildings. Heavy trucks rolled to and from the large pits, kicking up dust clouds to choke the air and lay a film on everything in sight. The din was unceasing, yet within the luxury car, only a low drone of the noise could be heard.

Nothing was as Alanna remembered it. There were no cheerful waves from the workers as had always met her father's appearance in the yard. No one indicated a desire to chat, even among themselves. Efficiency and work reigned. There wasn't time for anything else.

"You have't been here since your father sold, have

you?" Rolt observed as he parked the black Mark V in a reserved space.

"Only once, briefly," Alanna admitted coolly.

He switched off the motor but made no move to leave the car. "A lot has changed since your father's time, hasn't it?" He watched her, a considering look in his eyes. "I don't think you like the change, do you?"

Her violet eyes swept over the scene again. Guessing that he had somehow already read her thoughts or that she had betrayed them in her expression, Alanna gave a short negative shake of her head.

"We're making a profit, which is more than your father ever did," Rolt stated.

"I don't think I like it when a man's worth is measured by the amount of money he makes," she retorted.

The expectant gleam in his eyes, partially veiled by half-closed lashes, indicated that he had anticipated her response. She was left with the feeling that he had mockingly invited her remark.

"It's the challenge. Making something out of nothing or taking something that is dying and making it live again that brings satisfaction," he told her quietly. "It's fighting and winning. Money isn't the goal, it's the scoreboard. A man works to obtain his goal whether there's money at the end or not. It all comes back to the challenge."

"You sound like an authority on the subject," Alanna said in a frosty manner.

"Let's say that I always get what I want."

There was something faintly portentious about his statement that put Alanna instantly on guard. Suddenly the quiet elegance of the car seemed to close in around her. There were people everywhere around them, yet she didn't feel safe in the car with Rolt. Her pulse raced in silent alarm.

"This discussion is very enlightening, but I think I came here to see Kurt." The briskness of her reminder was brought on by her sudden attack of nervousness.

Her fingers closed over the door handle. She didn't want to wait in the car until Rolt walked around to open her door. Before she could release the latch, his hand had circled her wrist to hold her in the seat.

"Wait," he told her.

Alanna turned, apprehension rounding her eyes although she tried to conceal it. "Why?" She breathed the wary question.

Amusement glittered briefly in his eyes. She nearly flinched when his other hand moved, but its target was the sun visor above her head. Rolt flipped it down, revealing a lighted makeup mirror.

"You might want to do some repairs before you see Kurt." The gash near his mouth deepened into a mocking groove. "Unless you don't think he'll notice that your lipstick is smeared."

A scarlet stain dotted her cheeks as Alanna saw the smear of beige pink from her lips. He had deliberately waited until the last minute to point it out to her, thus forcing the memory of his kiss to the forefront just before she met Kurt.

Quickly she wiped away the smear with a tissue from her purse. Indigo blue eyes lazily watched her actions. His silent observation was unnerving, and her fingers began to tremble as she added fresh color to her mouth.

"Would you like me to blot it?" Rolt mocked.

"No, thank you." With hurried movements, she pressed the clean side of the tissue against her lips. "There," she said, indicating that she was finished and ready to leave the car.

"One more thing first," he insisted.

As he leaned towards her, Alanna tried to remain out of his reach, pressing her shoulders against the side of the car door. But it wasn't her arms that his hand sought, but the collar of her blouse.

"What are you doing?" she demanded, grabbing his wrists and trying to push his hands away from her blouse front. Anger at his effrontery banished any qualms.

Ignoring her attempts to keep him from his objective, he calmly unbuttoned the top button and moved to the second. She strained and pushed, but his strength was vastly superior to hers.

"Stop it!" she breathed angrily as the second button was set free.

Rolt merely smiled, if that mirthless movement of his mouth could be called a smile. The third button was released. With the thumb and forefinger of each hand, he opened the front into a vee, smoothing the material up to the collar, then down to the low point. There he stopped, his knuckles deliberately resting on the rounded swell of her breasts.

"I want you to look alluring for my brother." He surveyed his handiwork with satisfaction.

Heat flamed through her body at the way his gaze dwelt in the shadowy valley between her breasts. She trembled with impotent anger and embarrassment, her fingers locked on his wrists but no longer making any futile attempts to push his hands away. His attention lazily focused on her face.

"A little cleavage always arouses a man's interest," Rolt added.

His fingers seemed to burn through her blouse, branding their imprint on her soft flesh. "Take your hands off me!" Alanna demanded hoarsely.

With a patronizing tilt of his head in acquiesence, he let go of the material, deliberately trailing his fingertips over the pointed thrust of her breasts before straightening to his own side of the car.

The wicked glint in his eyes made Alanna wish she had a knife. She would have gladly plunged it into his heart at that moment and damned the consequences. Rolt opened the car door and stepped out, a rush of noise and dust racing in.

CHAPTER TWO

THE SPARKLE OF TEMPER was in her eyes, heightened color in her complexion. The tawny gold of her hair swung in soft curls about her neck, silken and shimmering. The flat of Rolt's hand rested proprietorially on the back of her waist as he guided her through the clerical department of the plant to his private office.

Alanna was aware of the interested and speculative glances they received from the employees, male and female. A few faces were familiar, but she doubted that they recognized her. Their main interest was the fact that their boss was escorting a young woman to his office.

Rolt obviously did not make a practice of entertaining women at the plant, and she wondered what they would think when they saw her with Kurt. They would probably conclude that she was playing one brother off against the other. If they only knew how uncomfortable the possessive hand on her back made her feel, they would appreciate the control she was exercising to keep from pushing it away.

A woman looked up from the typewriter as they walked through an office door. She was attractive in a plain sort of way, in her middle thirties. Unconsciously Alanna glanced at the wedding band on the woman's left hand before meeting the woman's curious gaze.

Rolt's hand shifted to her elbow, keeping Alanna at his side as he paused at the woman's desk. "Are there any messages, Mrs. Blake?"

"They're on your desk. Only one was urgent and it's on top," the woman answered in a crisp, professional tone.

He turned away, drawing Alanna awkwardly along towards a second door that obviously led to his inner sanctum. Over his sholder, he tossed out an order to his secretary. "Find Kurt and have him sent to my office right away."

There wasn't an opportunity for the secretary to acknowledge his request as he guided Alanna through the door and closed it behind him. His grip lessened and she immediately slipped free of the dreaded contact.

"Make yourself at home." His mouth quirked slightly as he moved farther into the room. "It will be a few minutes before Kurt arrives."

His strides took him away from her. Alanna breathed a bit easier and glanced around the office. It was hardly a typical office. The desk his secretary had referred to was not an accurate term since it resembled a table with a center drawer. A straight-backed chair and not an overstuffed leather chair sat behind it. It was definitely not something that a person would relax in and contemplate his successes. There were two or three other similar chairs situated near the table. Dark oak shelves covered one wall and a portion of a second. Books and papers abounded, but there were no cabinets.

The rest of the room was furnished with an enormous three-piece sectional sofa and equally sized knee-high table that followed its curving arc. The sofa was covered in a knobby material in variegated stripes of blue.

The drapes, covering the length of nearly one entire wall, were of the same material as the sofa. Beneath her feet, the carpet was a long, shaggy blue, plush and thick. Charcoal sketches of black and white adorned the remaining walls.

The decor was decidedly masculine and completely informal. It was so at odds with the other office areas Alanna had passed that she was stunned. It was not at all as she had imagined, and her expression revealed this.

"Is something the matter?" Rolt's amused voice inquired.

He was standing beside the desk, or table, which seemed the more appropriate term. The pink slips of telephone messages were in his hand. His lazily veiled look was inscrutable.

"You have to admit this is not your typical office," Alanna defended her astonishment. "Whoever heard of an executive without a massive walnut desk?" She couldn't keep a tinge of sarcasm from creeping into her voice, an after-effect of his previous treatment.

He laughed softly—more, Alanna thought, from her slightly spitting tone than from the content of her remark. Almost carelessly, he tossed the telephone messages on the table top.

"I have no need for drawers and compartments, but I do like a lot of flat working space. As for the rest of this—" Rolt scanned the large room impassively, dwelling briefly on the over-sized sofa that would have dwarfed any average living room "—it has a practical purpose, too. Department meetings can be held around the couch with the various papers and reports spread on the coffee table."

"You never do anything without a reason, do you?" she declared, and immediately wondered what his true reason had been for meeting her at the airport.

"I wouldn't say 'never,'" mocked Rolt, subtly reminding her of the last time he had reproved her usage of the word. "It is convenient, though, when the desire for creature comforts also fulfills a practical purpose."

"I wouldn't have guessed that you were vulnerable to human needs," Alanna replied tartly.

His gaze raked her with slow thoroughness from head to toe. "Do you doubt it?" his low voice inquired in a lazy, suggestive question.

Nearly fifteen feet separated them, yet the caress of his enigmatic blue eyes had been almost a physical touch. It was as if he had personally explored every intimate detail of her figure. Tension stretched between them, taut and vibrating, tingling down Alanna's nerve ends.

A slow warmth crept up her neck, and she turned away before it reached her cheeks and was revealed to his discerning gaze. She refused to make any comment to his suggestive question.

Seemingly of her own volition, her legs carried her forward, putting more distance between herself and Rolt. The closed drapes offered her a destination and she took it. Before her hand could lift the knobby material aside, the roll of a cord opened them.

Her startled look sought the reason and found Rolt, the thick carpet muffling his footsteps as he had joined her at the window. Quickly Alanna looked back to the window, her heart beating rapidly in unknown alarm.

"It's quite a view of the countryside when you can see it." His voice came from just over her right shoulder. Alanna stiffened, trying to judge how close he was to her without glancing around. Too close, her radar told her. "Unfortunately the dust usually leaves a film an inch thick on the glass. That's why I generally leave the drapes closed unless it's after a hard rain. It's a waste of time to have the windows washed."

The hazy view obscured the landscape, turning it into indefinable shapes and silhouettes. Yet Alanna's gaze remained steadfastly fixed on the dust-covered panes. The musky scent of his after-shave lotion

drifted in the air, nearly suffocating her with its heady
aroma. She longed to move away, but to turn in any
direction ultimately meant facing Rolt.

And Alanna felt uncomfortably vulnerable. It was
as if he knew the havoc he was wreaking on her
senses and delighted in shattering her poise. The
knowledge added fuel to her fire of dislike.

"How much longer will Kurt be?" she demanded
tersely.

"Does it matter?"

His hand touched her forearm. His intention was
obviously to turn her around, probably into his arms.
But Alanna was having none of it. Pivoting away from
his touch, she violently pushed his outstretched hand
away from her, eyes flashing her fury.

"Yes, it matters," she hissed. "If it will be very
much longer, I prefer to wait for him outside."

Rolt towered above her, strangely remote as he
looked down at her in a narrowed gaze. Inwardly intimidated by his poised attitude of retaliation, Alanna
didn't back down under his piercing look. A flicker of
a smile touched the corners of his mouth.

"That won't be necessary," he replied smoothly.
"He's cooled his heels long enough in the outer
office."

"He's here?" she breathed in frowning disbelief.

"Mrs. Blake notified me of his arrival a few minutes ago." There was a complacent gleam in his eyes.

That was impossible. She had been with him every
minute. "How?"

Briefly inclining his head, he indicated the table behind them. The movement highlighted the golden cast to his coffee-brown hair. "The small light illuminated on the telephone," he explained. "I dislike buzzers."

Her fingernails dug into the palms of her hands. "Do you mean Kurt has been out there all this time I've been waiting for him?"

"Not quite all of the time," Rolt qualified, and turned away to walk to the phone. Picking up the receiver, he punched a button and spoke into the mouthpiece. "You can send Kurt in now, Mrs. Blake."

The audacity of the man infuriated Alanna beyond measure. Strangled by her inability to express it, she could only glare at him. There was no time for any joyous anticipation of Kurt's arrival. The interconnecting office door opened and he walked in.

"You wanted to see me." Kurt's attention on entering was naturally focused first on Rolt. He was several feet inside the room before he noticed Alanna standing at the window. The handsomely masculine face was immediately wreathed in a beguiling smile. "Alanna!"

This was not the way she had visualized their meeting with her trembling in impotent rage at his brother, thus unable to respond with the same degree of gladness that had been in Kurt's voice.

"Hello, Kurt." Her answering smile was stiff and insincere.

He walked toward her, tall and darkly handsome, the light in his eyes warmly admiring. A part of her wanted to rush into his arms, knowing she would be welcomed, but she was too aware of the silent and mockingly observant Rolt. She didn't move, awkwardly waiting for Kurt to come to her.

"I'm sorry I wasn't able to meet you at the airport." His gaze inspected the lavender thunderclouds still lurking in the shadows of her eyes.

"It's all right." Alanna shook her head, trying to relax. "R—your brother explained the problem."

Unwillingly her gaze slid to Rolt. Some time during the course of her meeting with Kurt, Rolt had lit a cigarette. It was between his fingers, gray smoke curling to screen his look. There was something indolent about his stance, the tailored jacket thrust open by the hand in his pocket.

"I think the lady is waiting to be kissed, Kurt." His low voice traveled across the room to taunt Alanna.

"I don't need to be prompted," Kurt laughed softly, apparently finding nothing offensive in his older brother's remark, but then he wasn't aware of what had transpired at the airport.

Kurt's sunny blue gaze hadn't strayed from her face. It continued to beam on her as his hands closed over her shoulders and drew her toward him. He would never understand her desire to avoid the kiss and she was loath to have to explain. Under the circumstances, there seemed little else she could do but lift her head for his kiss.

The pressure of his mouth warmly covering her own would have been something she normally would have cherished and returned. As it was, with Rolt watching them with bold indifference to his intruder status, it was impossible for Alanna to respond except in the most half-hearted manner.

When Kurt lifted his head, there was a perplexed light in his gaze as he searched her face. Knowing he couldn't have failed to notice her lack of response to his kiss, she tried to sidetrack his attention from the fact.

A fingertip lightly touched a corner of his mouth. "I'm afraid you have lipstick all over you," Alanna stated in a contrite tone.

"I don't mind," he smiled.

"Here." Rolt's voice broke into their private conversaion. He moved to within a few feet of them, offering his linen handkerchief to Kurt. "Use mine. It's already soiled."

Both Alanna and Kurt glanced at the white cloth simultaneously. The beige-pink shade of her lipstick stained the material, contrasting sharply against the stark white. The freshness of her lipstick had probably smeared on Rolt's mouth too when he had forced his kiss on her, but Alanna had been too angry to notice. He had left her almost immediately to obtain her luggage. It must have been during his absence from her that he had used the handkerchief to wipe away her lipstick traces.

Rolt had given the same handkerchief to Kurt.

Realization flashed through Alanna that he had done it deliberately. In his own cunning way he had set up the incident, first prompting Alanna to freshen her makeup, then prompting Kurt to kiss her. Now he had produced the handkerchief to show his younger brother that he had kissed his girl.

As Kurt rather numbly took the handkerchief, his gaze riveted on the lipstick traces, Alanna sent Rolt a killing look. But his heart was encased in iron and it deflected her invisible daggers, leaving a bemused light in his hooded look.

Kurt rubbed the cloth over his mouth, briefly comparing the matching traces. Pride lifted Alanna's chin at the upward movement of his head. Bright with silent challenge, his questing gaze centered on Rolt. Rolt took the handkerchief from Kurt's hand.

"I stole a welcome home kiss at the airport," he stated calmly.

At least he didn't imply that she had given it freely, Alanna thought grimly. There was a thoughtful stillness about Kurt's expression as if he was still considering the information. Whatever his conclusion was, it wasn't written in his light blue eyes when he looked at Alanna. But she thought she deteced a faint tautness along his jaw line.

"Here's the keys to my car. Alanna's luggage is already in the trunk, so you might as well use it." Rolt tossed the keys to Kurt, lightning reflexes allowing him to catch them. "You'll want to take her home now."

"Yes, I will." Kurt's fingers closed over the keys, concealing them in the fist of his hand. An arm partially encompassed her shoulders to rest a hand between her shoulder blades.

Rolt moved toward his desk table as they turned to leave. "Before you go, Kurt, I want to give you fair warning." He picked up the telephone and punched out a series of numbers, not even bothering to glance at his brother as he spoke, nor at Alanna. "You've had a clear field with Alanna for long enough. Now I'm joining the competition."

Gasping, she couldn't believe that she had heard right. His boldness was unbelievable—he was talking about her as if she wasn't even in the room, then referring to her as if she was some prize to be won and not a human being capable of deciding for herself which man she preferred.

Hadn't she made it plain she heartily disliked him? And the audacity of telling his own brother that he was going after his girl! Alanna didn't know whether to unleash her temper or laugh at Rolt's limitless conceit.

Kurt, who had stiffened at the announcement, was evidently torn by conflicting reactions, too. He glared silently at the ruggedly carved profile Rolt presented to them.

The moment passed when either of them had an opportunity to respond. Rolt had reached the party he had dialed. "Hello, Sam. I have a message here that you called...."

Kurt's hand tightened on her shoulder. "Come on, let's go," he said gruffly.

The firm pressure of his hand on her back guided Alanna out of the office. She was as eager to leave as Kurt was. Neither spoke as they left the building. In the car, Kurt jammed the key in the ignition, then leaned back in the bucket seat without starting the motor.

"About what happened in there—" he sighed heavily.

"I know Rolt is your brother," Alanna interrupted, still influenced by her anger, "but he's the most overbearing, arrogant man I've ever met. Do you realize the way he maneuvered both of us?"

"I'm beginning to get a fairly good idea," he nodded, a dark brow arching upward in retrospection. His hands clenched the steering wheel, knuckles turning white under the fierceness of his grip. He gave her a sideways glance, alertly watchful. "He meant what he said, Alanna. I know him too well to doubt that."

"You mean about wanting me?" At Kurt's affirmative nod, she exhaled a contemptuous breath. "I can't stop him from trying, but he isn't going to get anywhere."

"Rolt attracts women the way flypaper attracts flies."

"This is one woman who's completely immune to his brand of primitive charm," Alanna declared emphatically.

"Everyone has violent feelings toward him one

way or another," Kurt insisted, "sometimes feeling both ways at the same time, including myself. But I don't think anyone can remain immune."

Alanna knew which category she fell in—the one feeling violently against Rolt. He had made a fiasco of her homecoming. Nothing had gone as she had planned. He had dominated nearly every second of it. Even now, she was sitting here alone in the car with Kurt and what were they talking about? Rolt.

Gazing at Kurt, so dark and so handsome, Alanna knew he was everything she had ever dreamed about. Rolt would never change that. He would never be able to come between them no matter how hard he tried. She was foolish to remain upset, nurturing her anger for him.

"I've missed you," she murmured. The shimmery fire of frustration became a glow of loving adoration as she gazed at Kurt.

A crooked smile slowly moved across his mouth. "Have you?" The troubled light was slow to leave the eyes that searched her face. Then one hand reached out to clasp hers. "I wanted to meet you at the airport," he declared huskily. "If only that damned equipment hadn't broken down, I would have."

"We can't change what's past." Alanna implied that it wasn't important any more. "But we can forget it and start from scratch."

"Yes, we can," Kurt agreed, "starting now."

He curved his other hand around the back of her neck and gently drew her half-way to meet him. A long, satisfying kiss claimed her lips and this time, without the disconcerting presence of his brother, she responded to it. When it was over, he remained close to nuzzle her cheek and tease the corners of her mouth.

"I could continue in this happy vein for much longer," he murmured softly, his warm breath caressing her skin. "But bucket seats are simply not designed for making love with any degree of comfort.' Lightly he kissed her lips once more and moved away. There was a wry twist of his mouth as he started the engine. "Of course I doubt that Rolt has made love in a car in a very long time."

Forget, she had said. Yet already Rolt's name had crept into the conversation. She sighed inwardly as she leaned back in her seat. Something told her that Rolt was not going to be an easy man to forget or ignore.

Irritatedly, she brushed a silky curl away from her cheek. The downward movement of her hand touched the collar of her blouse, and its gaping plunge to a vee immediately brought back the recollection of her struggle in this very same car with Rolt. Her flesh burned where he had insolently touched her. An angry resentment again rose inside her.

"Let's celebrate your homecoming tonight," Kurt stated as he drove out the gate. "I'll pick you up at six and we can get an early start. How's that?"

Alanna glanced at her watch, readjusting the direction of her thoughts. "It's my first night home. Mom and dad will expect me to spend some time with them."

"Make it seven, then," he compromised, sliding her a sparkling look. "You'll be home all summer. They can see you every day and I'll see you every night."

"Every night?" she teased.

"Well, I can't leave any free time open for Rolt to slip in," he stated. "He will be coming around, you know."

"He's going to be in for a very rude surprise if he does." There was a defiant tilt of her chin. "Because I'll show him the door so fast that he won't realize what's happened until it's over."

"I'd like to be there," Kurt laughed. "That would have to be a first for him."

Alanna joined his laughter, suddenly relaxing, no longer angered by Rolt's assertion that he would win her, only amused. There was vengeful pleasure as she anticipated the moment when she would tell him to get lost. She would enjoy dealing that blow to his male ego. It sorely needed deflating.

After their laughter had erased the subtle tension, it was easy for their conversation to switch to less disturbing topics. Alanna chattered happily away about the university, her exams and her plan for the summer vacation, not mentioning the large role she hoped Kurt would play in the latter.

Her high spirits at returning home were in full bloom when the car pulled into the driveway of her home. With a suitcase in hand and Kurt following with the rest, Alanna walked eagerly to the front door. It was opened before she had a chance to reach for the doorknob. A tall, spare woman stood within the white frame, her angular face wreathed in a smile of astonished delight.

"We didn't expect you until tomorrow!" she exclaimed.

"Hello, Ruth, I finished my exams a day early and caught the first flight out of Minneapolis," explained Alanna.

"You should have let us know," the woman remonstrated, giving her a quick hug before ushering her into the house and holding the door open for Kurt, laden with the rest of Alanna's suitcases.

"I wanted to surprise mom and dad." She glanced around the empty living room. "Where are they?"

"Your father is out playing some golf and Elinore is upstairs, resting before dinner." The housekeeper motioned for Kurt to set the bags inside the door.

"How is she?" Alanna's smile became slightly serious as she gazed earnestly at Ruth Ewell.

Referring to the woman as a housekeeper was really a misnomer. She had been hired first as a daily help when Alanna's mother had been expecting her. It had been doctor's orders that Elinore Powell do as little as possible, hoping to avoid the miscarriages that had ended her other three pregnancies.

During the months before and after Alanna's birth, her mother and Ruth Ewell had become friends. She had continued working for them on a daily basis until her husband passed away four years ago. At that time, Elinore had insisted that Ruth move in and live with them.

Because of the close, almost sister-like relationship between her mother and Ruth, Alanna had never looked on her as a domestic employee. She had become more of an adopted aunt than a paid housekeeper. Since her mother's stroke two years ago, Ruth had been the rock that held the household together.

"Her left arm is still a bit numb, but the doctor says she's doing nicely. Of course, Elly insists that she's as fit as a fiddle," Ruth confided in a skeptical tone, using her pet name for Alanna's mother. "But I notice she always lies down for a couple of hours in the afternoon, so she isn't as strong as she pretends." She waved a hand, slightly gnarled with arthritis, toward the living room. "You two go and make yourselves comfortable and I'll bring some coffee from the kitchen."

"Thanks anyway," Kurt shook his dark head regretfully, "but I'm afraid I'll have to pass. I'd better get back to work."

"Surely you can spare time for one cup," Ruth cajoled.

"No, I—"

"Ruth?" Elinore Powell's questioning voice came from the stairwell to the second floor. "Who's there?"

"It's Alanna and her young man." The answer was shouted back with a beaming smile on the couple. "She's come home a day early."

Alanna slid a sideways glance at Kurt, wondering if he minded being referred to as her young man. He caught the look and smiled at her gently, slipping an arm around her waist as if to reinforce the claim that they belonged together. A warm, pleasant feeling of being cared for stole over her. Soft contentment was etched in her expression as she turned to meet the petite woman gliding gracefully down the stairs.

Always fragile in appearance, Elinore Powell now looked even more delicate. Her heart had never been strong from childhood. Yet there was an aura of resiliency about her that led one to believe she could overcome anything, even ill health. There was a translucent quality to her complexion and an undiminished sparkle in her eyes. The silver gilt to her once blond hair added to her ephemeral loveliness.

"It's so good to have you home." Her mother's voice trembled with emotion as she embraced Alanna, a shimmer of happy tears in her ageless eyes. With innate grace, Elinore Powell turned to Kurt. "Were you an accomplice in Alanna's plot to surprise us?" she smiled.

"Yes," he nodded. "She phoned me."

"So you could meet her at the airport," Elinore concluded astutely. "I know it probably isn't necessary, but I want to thank you for meeting her and bringing her safely home." Alanna hesitated for an

instant, feeling the flick of Kurt's gaze on her, but she
didn't bother to correct her mother's impression that
Kurt had met her at the airport as planned. "I heard
Ruth mention coffee," her mother continued. "You
will stay for a few minutes, won't you, Kurt?"

"I really must get back to the plant," he refused a
second time. "We had some equipment problems this
afternoon. It was good seeing you again, Mrs. Powell,
and you too, Mrs. Ewell. Goodbye, Alanna." He bent
his head and unself-consciously brushed a light kiss
across her lips. "Seven?"

"I'll be ready," she promised.

With a polite nod at the two older women, he left.
Alanna didn't try to conceal the glow of pride in her
violet eyes. Kurt Matthews was a handsome, intelligent man. No girl could fail to feel proud if he was
interested in her. Her look was noted by both women,
who exchanged knowing glances.

"Why don't you bring that coffee into the living
room, Ruth," Elinore Powell suggested. "I'm sure
Alanna would like a cup after her flight. There's
plenty of time to unpack later."

Alanna had no objections to the idea. In truth, she
suddenly felt in need of a cup of coffee. So much had
happened since the plane touched down that a cup of
coffee seemed doubly inviting.

"Come on." Elinore Powell linked her arm with
her daughter's and led her toward the living room.
"You still haven't told me how you managed to leave
a day early."

Settled on the traditionally styled sofa of yellow and green print, Alanna explained about the last-minute rescheduling of her final exams and discussed how she felt she had done in the various classes, laughing with her mother and Ruth over some of the peculiarities of her professors. Then she had plied them with questions about what had been happening at home and for news of some of her former school chums, especially Jessie, Ruth's daughter. She and Jessie had been the closest friends, but Jessie had married almost immediately after high school graduation and moved out of state.

Through letters and Ruth, they had still kept in touch.

Jessie had recently sent a group of snapshots of her and her family and Ruth quite proudly showed them to Alanna. "Here's Jessie with little Amy. She's three months old there. Isn't she a little doll, with that button nose and dark hair?" Alanna agreed and was handed another photograph. "That's Mikey. He's growing so fast. Jessie said in her letter that he's a typical terrible two-year-old."

Gazing at the photographs, Alanna couldn't help thinking how very happy Jessie looked. There was a positive bloom about her cheeks, especially in the photograph where she was holding the baby and looking at her husband John. Alanna didn't know him very well, but he was a good-looking man in a solid sort of way.

Theirs had been a whirlwind courtship and radiant

was the only way to describe Jessie after three years of marriage. Alanna hoped that was the way it would be for her, too. She tried to visualize a picture of herself and Kurt. But before the image could form, Ruth was speaking again.

"Now that they have a healthy boy and girl, Jessie thinks the family will be complete with no more additions. Sam and Andrew each have four, but she has no intention of trying to keep up with her brothers," Ruth stated, referring to her sons. The mantel clock in the dining room chimed. "Heavens!" Ruth exclaimed. "If we're going to eat dinner at a decent hour, I'd better get started."

"I'll help," Mrs. Powell offered, starting to rise from the sofa as Ruth straightened.

"You stay here and talk to Alanna," the woman admonished firmly. "You haven't seen her since Easter."

"If you need me, just call." Her mother didn't pursue her offer and Alanna was reminded of her shaky health.

As Ruth left the room, she turned her attention back to the photographs, but her thoughts were on her mother. It was still difficult to accept after all this time that her mother's activities were limited. She still exuded a vitality that belied her weakness. A sigh came from her mother, wistfully sad, drawing Alanna's gaze.

"Is something wrong, Mother?"

"Not really," she smiled. "I was just wondering

how long it would be before I'll be able to show off pictures of my grandchildren. Or even if I'll be around to see them born."

"Oh, Mother, don't talk that way," Alanna murmured with a catch in her voice.

"I wasn't referring to an early demise," Elinore laughed, a bright melodious sound. "My dear, since you turned sixteen, there's been a string of male admirers knocking at our door and you haven't taken one of them seriously. Are you going to become one of those modern career women? Not that I don't think a woman should have a career, but selfishly I keep hoping that you might be able to include a husband and family in your life, too."

"I'm twenty-one. That practically makes me an old maid, doesn't it?" Alanna teased, relief flowing through her that her mother had maintained her optimistic grasp on the future.

"Seriously, Alanna," her mother smiled, "what about Kurt Matthews? Is he the one? Are you in love with him?"

A momentary stillness swept over her. She looked down at the pictures in her hand. "I think so," she nodded.

"Think so?" Disappointment and affection ran through the responding voice. "My dear, I doubt if it's love if you only think so. When you're in love with a man, he either makes you so impossibly angry that you can't think straight or he transports you to some heavenly plateau."

"Is that right?" There was an impish light in her eyes as she glanced at her mother. "Is that the way dad makes you feel?"

"After thirty years, he still has the power to exasperate me beyond endurance," Elinore Powell admitted laughingly. "But the heavenly plateau has become much more solid and lasting. I think it's something that exists only in the sweet romance of courtship. Which is just as well, because it isn't wise to go through life with your head in the clouds all the time."

Alanna smiled and nodded. Secretly she thought her mother's idea about love was a bit old-fashioned and sentimental. Love wasn't like that today, probably it never had been except in romantic dreams. Love wasn't something that happened. It was something that grew out of genuine affection and admiration into something more solid. But she didn't voice her opinion. There was no reason to debate the point.

CHAPTER THREE

IT SEEMED TO ALANNA that her father was a bit preoccupied during dinner that evening. His eyes kept straying to his wife whenever he felt she was looking at him, and there was a faintly troubled light in his eyes and a certain tension about his finely chiseled mouth. It seemed to accent the aging lines in his handsome, sensitive face. His hair was iron-gray, receding at the temples, yet still giving the impression of being thickly full.

They were such a perfect couple, Alanna thought, not for the first time. They were so devoted to each other, each more concerned about the other's wants and needs than their own. Perhaps that was what was bothering her father now. She knew her mother's health was poor, but maybe he had detected something in her manner tonight that gave him cause to worry. He would be more apt to see it since Alanna had been away and wouldn't be able to discern any small change. She studied her mother circumspectly, trying to see her through her father's eyes, but she noticed nothing.

"Oh, Dorian," Ruth looked up from her plate, "I

called the plumber. He'll be over tomorrow morning to see what's the matter with the pipes in the laundry room. I meant to tell you earlier and forgot."

Her father sighed heavily. "I'm beginning to think we should have all new plumbing installed. First it was the upstairs bathroom; then it was the kitchen. Now the laundry room." He shook his head. "There's only the downstairs bathroom left."

"The house is old," her mother pointed out. "You can't expect it to last forever."

"I'm beginning to think it's become a white elephant." He made a studious job out of slicing a mouth-size portion of roast beef on his plate. "I was golfing today with Bob Jackson—he's the one with the real estate firm," he added in explanation. "He was telling me that there's quite a demand for housing these days, especially homes located in our area. He seems to think it would fetch a handsome price if we put it on the market."

"You aren't thinking of selling, are you, Dorian?" Her mother laid her silverware on the table and stared at him in disbelief.

"We aren't getting any younger, Elinore," he said, not meeting her gaze. "With Alanna away at college most of the year, this house is really too big for our needs. The upkeep and expense of running it is getting out of hand—the plumbing, and we're going to need a new roof before winter. We could sell it and buy us a nice condominium with money left over to put in the bank. We wouldn't have to worry any more about heating empty rooms or shoveling snow, raking leaves, or mowing lawns. Let's be honest. This house is beginning to be a burden."

"Dorian Maxwell Powell, I don't want to hear another word!" her mother exclaimed.

"Would you sell it?" Alanna breathed, her throat constricting at the idea of strangers living in her home.

"He is not going to sell it!" Elinore stated emphatically.

"I never said I was," he placated. "I was only pointing out that it would be the practical thing to do."

"I don't care if it's practical or not," her mother retorted. She picked up her knife and fork again. "I don't see how you could even suggest such a thing. You were born in this house. It was built to your father's specifications down to the last detail. It would be like selling your heritage. How could you even consider such a thing?"

"Now, now Elinore, don't get so upset," he soothed with an apologetic smile. "I just thought that this big old house might be getting too much for you and Ruth to take care of and I didn't want....Well," he faltered, choosing his words with care, "if you wanted something smaller, I thought you might not say so because of the very reasons you mentioned."

"Oh, darling." Elinore bit her lip, touched by his gesture. "This is our home. It always has been and it always will be if I have any say about it."

"Of course you do," he smiled. "I guess it was foolish of me to bring it up."

"It certainly was," Elinore sniffed.

And Alanna smiled, marveling again at the selfless consideration her parents showed for each other. She glanced at her watch.

It was after six. She wouldn't have much time to get ready before Kurt arrived.

"I'm going to have to skip dessert if I want to be ready when Kurt gets here," she declared.

"But I've done your favorite," Ruth protested. "Fresh strawberries and baking powder biscuits with thick cream from the Johanson farm."

Alanna grimaced regretfully. "Save me some. I'll have it for breakfast in the morning."

"You shouldn't be eating dessert for breakfast," Ruth said in a disapproving tone.

"Why not? It isn't any different from having fresh fruit and toast," she teased.

Cleaning her plate, she asked to be excused and hurried to her room. By the time she had showered, applied fresh makeup, and changed, Kurt was already there. She could hear him in the living room talking to her mother as she came down the stairs. Her father stepped out of the library and paused when he saw her. His serious expression softened at the sight of her.

"You look lovely, Alanna." Dorian Powell walked to the foot of the stairs to meet her. His gaze ran over her, admiring the amethyst sparkle the lavender dress gave to her eyes. "Even if I am a bit prejudiced it's still the truth."

"Thank you, daddy." She kissed him lightly on the cheek and glanced toward the living room. "Has Kurt been waiting long?"

"No more than five minutes, but once he sees you he won't mind," he answered, smiling. "Tell me, are you serious about young Matthews? Should I be in there interrogating him like a future father-in-law?"

Twice in one day—first her mother and now her father! Alanna couldn't believe it. She laughed with a trace of bewilderment.

"You're as bad as mother," she declared. "You both seem intent on whisking me off to the altar. I have a year of college to finish yet."

Pain flickered briefly in his eyes. "Of course you do," he repeated, a chagrined smile touching his mouth. "Your mother and I are just naturally anxious to know that your future is secure, that there's someone around who will love you and look after you the way we do."

"I'm capable of looking after myself," Alanna reminded him gently.

"I know that, honey," her father nodded. "But I guess parents always think about their daughter getting married to some nice young man who'll be able to provide a good home for her. To me, Rolt's brother seems like an ideal prospect. He's pleasant and intelligent and I know Rolt will always look out for his interests."

And how! Alanna thought. It was on the tip of her tongue to tell her father exactly what kind of brother Kurt had. Look out for Kurt's interest, indeed! How much would her father admire Rolt if he found out that Rolt was planning to try to steal her away from his brother?

She swallowed back the words. It would only upset her father to have his confidence in Rolt shaken. He would start worrying about the plant and all the employees and their families who depended on it.

"I think Kurt can take care of himself without any help from his brother," she said instead.

"Probably he can," her father conceded, but in a doubtful tone that irritated Alanna. "Young Matthews could get ahead on his own, but he doesn't have the drive that Rolt does. After all, Rolt is—"

"—a giant. I know, daddy." She sighed. "The next thing I know you'll be advocating that I marry Rolt."

"Well. . . ." An impish twinkle danced in his eyes. But Alanna failed to find it amusing and the light faded from his eyes. "When you do marry, I only want it to be to the man you want," he added.

"I know." A rueful smile curved the vulnerable line of her mouth. No matter what he said, she knew he simply wanted her to be happy. Parents just had odd ideas sometimes about what would make their children happy. "I'd better not keep Kurt waiting any longer," she declared, and gave her father a quick hug because she loved him. "Don't wait up for me."

He smiled as she moved toward the living room.

Alanna thought his sensitive face looked sad and troubled behind the cheerful smile. Fleetingly she wondered why, then Kurt was rising to meet her and she didn't have time to contemplate the cause.

Several times during the rest of the week the impression returned. It wasn't anything Alanna could put her finger on, but the sensation that something was wrong wouldn't go away. It was like a dark cloud lurking near the sun, casting a shadow without dimming the light.

Once, when her mother was napping and they were alone, Alanna had voiced her concern. They were sitting in the living room, her father staring off into space in a preoccupied fashion.

"What's wrong, dad?" she had asked.

"Hmm? What?" He had looked at her blankly, not catching the question.

"Is something wrong? You look as if you have some deep, dark problem weighing you down," Alanna had teased, making light of her serious question.

"Old age," he had sighed, his mouth quirking.

"Oh, you're not old," she had protested, but a quick mental calculation reminded her that he was nearly sixty.

"Sometimes I feel very old—and tired."

But he still hadn't answered her question and Alanna had probed further. "Is it mother? Are you worried about her?"

His light brows drew together in a line of hurt. "I

can't help worrying about her, Alanna." He had reached out and clasped her hand. "I love her."

"I know, daddy." She had squeezed his hand affectionately. "So do I."

"It's hard to accept that life doesn't go the way we hope or even plan that it will." He had stared again into space. "Your mother and I had such plans for our retirement. There was so much I wanted to do for her and show her."

His voice had trailed off, but Alanna had finished the unspoken thought. Her mother's weak heart had ended those plans. Disappointment and regret now plagued her father.

"But she has you, daddy," Alanna had pointed out. "And that's what she wants most of all."

"Yes," he had nodded absently, but the look in his eyes had said that he wanted to give her much more.

It troubled him that her health wouldn't permit the traveling and activities they had once planned. And Alanna guessed that he regretted not doing much of it earlier when her mother had been able to take part.

"There's no sense letting it upset you, dad," she had murmured.

He hadn't replied and Alanna had let the subject drop.

But it had eased her mind. She watched them now, her father hovering, her mother protesting, and couldn't help smiling.

"I think you should wear a hat," her father was saying. "The sun can be pretty hot."

"I'm not made of ice cream. I won't melt in the sun," Elinore Powell insisted in exasperation. "I'll sit in the shade if it gets too warm."

"I think I'll put a hat in the car just in case," he decided.

Elinore glanced at Alanna and smiled, shaking her head at the hopelessness of arguing with him. "Are you sure you don't want to join us for Sunday dinner? Ruth fixed a delicious picnic lunch."

"Two's a company and three's a crowd," Alanna quipped. "Besides, Kurt will be over at four o'clock. There isn't any need for you and Dad to cut your afternoon short just to bring me back here."

"It doesn't seem right to leave you here alone on your first Sunday home," her mother sighed.

"Don't worry about it," she insisted. "I'm going to have a quiet, relaxing afternoon. I have a good book to read and I'm going to lie in the sun and read it."

"Well, if you're sure," her mother said grudgingly.

"Mother, if you're not careful, you're going to turn into a mother hen like dad!" Alanna laughed.

"Heaven forbid!" The answering response joined her laughter.

A few moments later, her parents were gone. With her book under one arm and the portable radio in the other hand, Alanna wandered out onto the patio at the back of the house. The concreted area was almost the only section of the vast lawn to receive the afternoon sun. Large pine trees and one maple tree shaded the rest.

Redwood lawn furniture was scattered in casual order about the patio. Setting the radio on a circular redwood table, Alanna slipped out of her cotton beach jacket and tossed it on a nearby chair. Her brief bikini matched the jacket, a bold print of crimson and gold. She tuned the radio to a station that played a combination of popular music and old standards, then settled on to the redwood chaise lounge.

Reaching behind her neck, she untied the halter straps of her bikini top and let them fall to her side to avoid the white stripes they would make as the rest of her skin tanned. The neighboring homes were some distance away, separated by the vast lawns, so she was not concerned about any prying eyes. With sunglasses protecting her eyes from the glare of the sun, she opened her book and began reading, quickly becoming engrossed in the historical saga.

"Beautiful." A male voice murmured the compliment.

Alanna glanced up, startled. Between the radio music and her own absorption in the novel, she had not heard the sound of anyone's approach. But there, a few feet from her chair, towered Rolt Matthews. She had not seen nor heard from him since the day she had arrived in Hibbing. Because of that, she had begun to discount his statement that she would be the recipient of his attention whether she wanted to be or not, and that mistake in judgment had lulled her into a false sense of security.

Stunned, her mouth refused to function. She stared

at him, momentarily unable to speak. He was dressed
casually, the clinging print material of his shirt complementing the light blue of his snug-fitting trousers.
The breadth of his masculine chest was outlined by
the shirt, accenting the tapering length to his waist.
Half of the buttons were unfastened, revealing
golden-brown hairs curling against the tan of his hard
flesh. A gentle breeze rippled through his thick brown
hair, which was gilded by the sunlight. There was a
sensual twist to his mouth.

He took a step forward, and his movement finally
spurred her into speech. "How did you get here?"
she asked him angrily.

"No one answered the door. I heard the radio playing and came around to investigate."

The direction of his hooded gaze made Alanna suddenly aware of the bikini strings hanging freely at her
sides, and of how much the loosened top exposed of
the full curves of her breasts. The book was discarded
as she quickly gathered the strings and tied them
around her neck.

Swinging her feet to the sun-warmed concrete of
the patio, she stood up. The brief swimsuit made her
feel too naked, but her beach jacket was lying on the
chair Rolt was standing beside.

"Would you please leave? I have no wish to see
you," she said with the greatest difficulty in sounding
composed and controlled.

Rolt ignored the taut request. "I noticed your parents' car is gone. Your housekeeper is off for the day,

too, isn't she?" He reached down and picked up her beach jacket, holding it in his hand. His gaze raked her soft curves.

Alanna's skin burned. A slow warmth began to rise in her neck. She wanted the jacket desperately, to conceal her figure from his insolent blue eyes, but not for anything would she ask him to give it to her.

"Go away, Rolt." She tossed her head back in proud defiance.

"And leave you here alone to entertain yourself? I couldn't do that," he mocked.

"If you don't leave, I'll call the police," Alanna threatened.

"Will you?" he returned smoothly, and she realized that to get to the house and the telephone, she would have to pass him. It didn't take much intuition to know he wouldn't let her by to fulfil that threat.

"So help me, if you don't leave," she sputtered angrily, "I'll scream!"

"Go ahead." His gaze centered on the moistness of her lips. "I would enjoy silencing your cries."

Alanna inhaled sharply and about-faced, trembling with rage. How she would love to defy him and scream her head off, but the thought of his hard mouth smothering her lips was a strong deterrent.

"Why do you stay when you know how much I despise you?" she demanded in a strangled voice.

"I find you attractive and desirable," Rolt stated.

"Even though I'm going with your brother? You don't feel guilty about that at all, do you?"

"I've decided that I don't want you for a future sister-in-law. I want you for myself."

"But I don't want you!" Alanna cried in irritation. Suddenly she was still as a thought occurred to her. She tipped her head to one side and gazed at him. "Or is that it? You know I don't like you and you find that a challenge, don't you?"

The indigo shade of his eyes deepened, concealing his thoughts in dark, unreadable pools. "Perhaps." His aloof voice made it neither a yes or a no.

"That's it, isn't it?" She felt certain she was right. "I'm a challenge to your over-inflated ego. Because I prefer your brother to a cold fish like you."

"Cold?" An eyebrow arched in arrogant mockery.

"Yes, cold," Alanna repeated forcefully. "Cold and insensitive. You have no feelings, no compassion for anyone but yourself. Not even your brother."

His mouth thinned. "Then how do you explain the way I feel toward you?"

"You're the fox and I'm the grapes just out of reach. Emotions don't enter into it, otherwise you wouldn't be here when you know I don't like you at all."

"Maybe I want to change your mind," Rolt suggested.

"You'll never do that!" Alanna said angrily.

"You aren't meant for my brother. You're mine." There was a gleam of fierce possession in his eyes. "He would never make you happy."

"And you would, I suppose," she jeered.

"I would make you very happy," he stated with complete certainty.

Alanna turned her head away, seething at his unbelievable conceit. A thousand angry words ran through her mind, spiteful phrases of how contemptible she found his arrogance. All of them churned inside waiting to be hurled at him in a torrent of temper. Yet the scathing words would not deal the crippling blow that she longed for. There was another way, however, that she might accomplish it.

She glanced at him over her shoulder, her gaze wary and skeptical. "Forgive me if I find that hard to believe. How could you possibly be so certain when you hardly know me?"

His gaze narrowed, measuring. "I think I know you better than you do."

"Really?" Alanna taunted in doubting sarcasm. Deliberately she moved toward him, coming nearer to stand in front of him, tilting her head back to meet the full force of his gaze. Her heart beat faster. Her plan was daring and dangerous. "Then why don't I like you?"

"Because you're afraid," Rolt answered easily. "You're afraid of me and of yourself."

For a moment his reply disconcerted her. Bewilderment glittering briefly in her violet eyes. She quickly concealed it, but not before it had been noticed by Rolt.

"I'm not afraid of you," she denied, "and I'm certainly not afraid of myself."

"Aren't you?" His mouth curved in amusement, faintly superior and mocking.

"No."

The gleam in his eye plainly laughed at her answer. Alanna breathed in, controlling her anger. Then she thoughtfully nibbled on her lower lip, peering at him through the sweep of her lashes. Gathering her courage, she reached out, letting her fingers touch the opened front of his shirt. She felt him stiffen and a tingle of approaching victory ran through her nerve ends.

"I'm not afraid of you," she repeated, slowly letting her fingers travel up his shirt to the collar.

Standing on tiptoe, she lifted her head toward the ruthless line of his mouth. Rolt waited, not moving even when her lips lightly touched his. Alanna swayed closer, her hands curving around the strong column of his neck. His own hands settled on the bare curve of her waist, resting there without actually holding her.

As the kiss lengthened, Alanna felt his mouth moving mobilely in response, deepening with desire. Feigning reluctance, she disentangled her suddenly trembling lips from his, but she made no attempt to move away from him, letting his hands remain on her waist while her head rested on the granite solidness of his chest. A light blazed darkly in his eyes, sensual and seductive, partially screened by his thick lashes.

His head dipped slowly toward her. Alanna checked the movement with fingertips pressed against his mouth and a small negative shake of her head. Rolt didn't argue or force the issue, waiting, the disturbing look not leaving his gaze.

"You see, I'm not afraid of you," she murmured. Strength of purpose kept her immune from his male virility. For a few seconds more, she kept her eyes blank and expressionless. "Do you know why I kissed you?" Her fingers drifted back to his chest.

"Why?" His voice was even, faintly amused, not revealing any of the passion blazing so vividly through the veil of his masculine lashes. His control was superb.

"Because—" her gaze fell from his as she breathed in to control a tremor of temper "—I wanted you to know what I feel for your brother I could never feel for you. It's not your kisses I want, it's his. Not your arms and not your touch. I will never be yours because I find you disgusting!"

Intense hatred flamed through her voice as she finished her speech. On the concluding word, she started to wrench free from his unresisting touch, but her scathing words had not left him stunned as she had expected.

His hands left her waist, but only to grip the soft flesh of her upper arms and jerk her against him. Immediately his arms encircled her, crushing her in an iron vice, trapping her arms between their bodies. Alanna writhed and twisted in the trap, straining to be free.

Harsh, low laughter mocked her futile attempts.

She stopped struggling, knowing it was no use, and tossed her head back to glare at him coldly.

His eyes were hard, the line of his mouth more ruthlessly drawn than ever. Her blow had not crippled him, it had aroused his wrath. The silent fury of it caught at Alanna's breath and she was immediately angry with herself for letting it intimidate her.

"Never?" Rolt taunted in a low sneer.

Before she could elude him, her mouth was imprisoned by the burning force of his. It denied her breath as it consumed and destroyed, shattering her illusion that a kiss was an act of love and affection. Controlled savagery marked his possession, dominating her until she felt the acid taste of surrender on her moist lips. She strained, fighting the crush of his arms, but the hard circle held her fast.

Her bare legs carried the imprint of the tight weave of his slacks. Muscular thighs, like solid rock columns, pressed hotly against her flesh. The pinning arms had forced her spine to arch, molding her skin, her senses already swamped by the heady, musky scent of him, blood pounding in her ears.

The cruel mouth released her swollen lips, which were throbbing now in quivering disbelief. Alanna breathed in shuddering gasps, her head bowed in acknowledgment of the superior force of the onslaught and her inability to fend it off. The ignominy of her defeat burned in her cheeks.

One arm of the vice moved away. The freed hand punishingly gripped her throat, forcing her chin up.

Resentment flared violescent in her eyes that Rolt should inspect the extent of his victory. The bronze mask of his malely harsh features bore no trace of the primitive ravishment he had inflicted. Yet dark, intimidating fires still blazed in the cold blue of his eyes.

"I hate you!" Her words were half strangled by his choking fingers and the bitter sob that rose in her throat.

"Hate me if you want." The grooves near his mouth deepened sardonically. Her feelings or emotions didn't interest him, she realized again. "But you will be mine."

"No!" She had nearly said never, but she doubted she could withstand him a second time. Her walls were yet intact and she didn't want to risk having them breached.

"Yes, my Alanna." The possessive ring in his voice chilled her with its certainty. Rolt laughed softly, mockingly, at the uncontrollable shiver that danced over her shoulders. "Remember that when Kurt kisses you. Because soon you will know only mine and his will be a fading memory. It is my ring you will wear on your finger. When you lie naked in bed beside your husband, the man will be me. No one else."

Her heart leapt in fear. The low, mesmerizing voice was painting a picture that Alanna could see all too clearly. It was as if she was looking into the future and seeing her fate written in the indigo glitter of his gaze.

Her head made a tiny movement of protest. His fingers relaxed their grip on her throat as if knowing she was incapable of looking away. The hand traveled down the slender curve of her neck to cover her breast, her heart hammering madly against it.

"I will be the one to caress you, Alanna," Rolt continued huskily, "the one to learn your intimate secrets. It will be my name you will whisper in the night." An inarticulate sound came from her throat, almost a surrender, and satisfaction glimmered through his impassive mask. "Your eyes tell me that you think it might be true. It is true. You will find it out—in time."

Then he released her completely. Alanna swayed unsteadily. She felt hot and cold at the same time, numb with shock yet every nerve alive. The ambivalence of her reaction was frightening. She stared sightlessly at the patio floor, trying to understand how she could feel so many things at the same time.

Something was wrapped around her shoulders, and she glanced up, dazed. The beach jacket covered her bikini, providing her protection too late. Rolt was standing beside her, watching her. Blankly she met his enigmatic look.

"I want you to have dinner with me tomorrow night," he stated.

For a moment she could only stare at him, still lost in her split world. Rising like a phoenix from the ashes, her will surfaced.

"No," she refused flatly.

Rolt shrugged, as if to say it was only a matter of time, and accepted her decision. When he spoke, his voice was soft yet very clear, quietly unrelenting. "Don't forget what I've told you."

Alanna covered her ears with her hands. "Get out of here!" she shouted hoarsely.

Her eyes were tightly closed, trying to shut out the picture he had painted so indelibly. Rolt left the patio as quietly as he had come. Alanna's position didn't vary, not until the distant sound of a motor turning over in the driveway reached her muffled hearing. With a broken sob, she slumped on to the chaise lounge, but she didn't cry. There was too much anger, frustration, and confusion for tears.

Nothing he said was possible, she kept telling herself. He couldn't make her marry him against her will. It was only the momentary spell he had woven that had allowed her to believe it for a few frightened seconds. None of it could come true without her consent. And she would never give it. Never!

CHAPTER FOUR

THE PORCHLIGHT dimly illuminated the front door. The night air was scented by the ever-present, pervasive perfume of pines. Crickets and cicadas droned endlessly. The little traffic on the street at that late hour was far away.

In the shadows cast by the porchlight, Kurt's kiss deepened with persuasive ardor. It wasn't his kiss that Alanna experienced. Unwanted, unbidden, the brutal mastery of Rolt's kiss rocked her senses. The memory returned so suddenly, so unexpectedly, that she violently wrenched away from Kurt's embrace. When she saw the puzzled blue of his eyes instead of the indigo glitter of Rolt's, she realized what she had done.

"What's the matter? What have I done?" Bewildered laughter laced his voice.

Alanna turned away, taut, unable to meet his searching gaze. "It's...it's nothing." A trace of irritation at her own behavior accompanied her faltering denial of any wrongdoing on Kurt's part.

"Something is wrong," he insisted, his hands turning her tense shoulders around so she faced him.

"Tell me what it is," he coaxed gently. She looked into his handsome features, and a wave of hopelessness washed over her. There wasn't any way she could tell Kurt about Rolt's visit this afternoon or explain the way it had affected her.

She tilted her head back, moving it in a weary, negative motion. "I—I have a slight headache."

That had to be the oldest excuse on record, but Kurt had no reason to question her statement. He accepted it at face value and smiled ruefully.

"You should have said something earlier," he told her.

"I didn't want to spoil our evening," Alanna said.

"You probably got too much sun this afternoon," Kurt suggested.

Too much Rolt, she thought grimly. "Perhaps," she conceded with a brief nod.

"I don't want to let you go in, but I guess I'd better. I'll call you tomorrow, okay?" His dark head was tipped to one side.

"Yes," Alanna agreed, and lifted her mouth for his good-night kiss.

He brushed her lips lightly, but they remained cool and untouched by his gentleness. The memory of Rolt overshadowed the reality of the moment, spoiling any pleasure she might have obtained from Kurt's caress.

Inside the house, she leaned against the closed front door, shutting her eyes for a brief instant. *Don't forget,* Rolt had said. He needn't have bothered, she thought bitterly. He had successfully come between her and Kurt tonight, and she had the uneasy feeling it wasn't going to be the last time that it would happen.

Around ten the next morning, the telephone rang. Alanna was closest, so she answered it. "Powell residence. Alanna speaking," she said automatically.

"How's your headache?"

Her first thought was that it was Kurt phoning as promised. "All gone," she replied with forced lightness. The low mocking laughter that followed her words made her realize her mistake. It was Rolt. "How did you know about that?" she breathed angrily.

"When I saw Kurt this morning, I couldn't help commenting on how rested he looked. He explained that he'd had an early night last night because you'd had a headache." His taunting voice laughed at her excuse.

"Why did you call, Rolt?" she demanded.

"Do I have to have a reason?"

"No, but I'm sure you do." And it was probably to gloat.

"Maybe I wanted to hear your voice."

●"Well, I hope you enjoy hearing this." Alanna slammed the receiver on the hook, wishing she had broken his eardrums and doubting if she could be that lucky.

She glowered for a second longer at the telephone, then pivoted away.

Her mother was watching her, a bemused twinkle in her eyes.

"Was that Rolt Matthews on the phone?" she inquired.

"Yes." Alanna's answer was abrupt, a leftover piece of her temper.

"I was wondering when he would get around to calling," Elinore Powell commented with a knowing tilt of her head.

"What made you think Rolt would call?" She was wary and on edge.

"Remember when he and Kurt were over here during Easter? Well, I could tell by the way Rolt kept watching you that he was interested. You were probably too wrapped up in Kurt to notice, but I did," her mother declared.

"Well, I can't stand him!" Alanna snapped.

"He makes you angry, does he?"

"Yes! He's—" She stopped short, suddenly recognizing the sparkle in her mother's eye, and guessing its cause. "And don't look at me that way, mother," she declared impatiently. "It's not what you're thinking. He may enrage me, but he will never raise me to some heavenly plateau!"

She spun away and raced blindly from the room. Even her own mother was going over to the enemy camp!

She railed against the unfairness of it. Rolt cast a long shadow, a giant's shadow, and it seemed to be looming over more and more of her life.

DURING THE REST OF THE WEEK, Rolt didn't attempt to make any further direct contact with Alanna. He didn't have to, since he had managed to interfere quite successfully in one way or another. Twice she had seen him briefly when she was with Kurt, and her parents had invited him over for dinner one evening. Luckily it had been an evening she had already planned to spend with Kurt.

Most of the time it was simply the thought of him that disturbed her. Each time she was with Kurt, Alanna would remember that afternoon and the things that Rolt had said and done. She couldn't forget them. She couldn't relax with Kurt. When he touched her or held her, she kept measuring her reaction, wanting to avoid a repetition of that night on the porch. In consequence, she was tense and unnatural. To cover it, she became overly friendly and affectionate to prove to herself as well as to Kurt how much she cared for him.

With her fingers twined in his, she led Kurt from the dance floor to their small table in the crowded bar, laughing over her shoulder into his handsome face. Saturday night had filled the bar with people, and their voices and laughter made it difficult to hear the music of a local band. Not that it really mattered. Everyone was there to have fun. Music was the background.

White slacks and a white tunic was not perfect choice of clothes to wear in these crowded circumstances, but Alanna knew it set off her slim figure and the light golden tan she had acquired. And the silk

underblouse of swirling lavenders and grays highlighted the unusual violet shade of her eyes. In this
carefree atmosphere she felt quite bewitching.

The ardent glow in Kurt's eyes seemed to affirm
that he was definitely under her spell. He didn't release her hand as they reclaimed the chairs they had
vacated to dance. Their chairs were drawn close together so that their shoulders touched.

Kurt leaned over and nuzzled the tawny curls near
her ear lobe. "I love you, Alanna," he murmured
huskily. He drew back a few inches, a faint look of
wonder in his eyes as if he was surprised by the words
he had spoken. "I love you, Alanna," he repeated
with conviction.

She had been waiting for those words since Easter.
Now, more than ever before, they made her feel safe.
Rolt's threats became meaningless, and her spirits
soared with the release.

"I love you, too, Kurt," she said with genuine
warmth.

"It's a crazy place to tell you." His gaze swept the
noisy room briefly before returning to her face.

"It's a wonderful place," she protested softly.

"We've known each other for—how long?—A
month?"

"About that."

Of course, people have fallen in love in less time
than that, haven't they?" Kurt reasoned away the
shortness.

"A lot less," agreed Alanna.

"We should be in some luxurious restaurant, drinking champagne." He shook his dark head.

"In Minnesota?" Alanna teased.

"Yes, in Minnesota," Kurt grinned. "That's where I should have taken you tonight instead of here. Or I should have waited to tell you until we were alone."

"Does it matter?" She tipped her head to one side, lips parting in an invitation. "I mean, does it really matter where we are?"

"Not if you say you love me again."

"I love you."

"Alanna!" He breathed her name in a caress as his mouth descended toward the promise of hers.

"Kurt—Alanna. What a surprise to find the two of you here." Rolt's dryly mocking voice separated them instantly. "I would have thought you'd take Alanna to some place less public."

Alanna's head was up, as if scenting danger. That moment of feeling secure and safe was gone. She no longer was certain that Kurt's love would be able to protect her. Not from Rolt.

"At the time, it seemed a likely spot. It's only now that I'm beginning to see its disadvantages," Kurt conceded. Alanna felt his smiling look and briefly returned a strained imitation of it.

"What are you doing here, Rolt?" The flash of her eyes accused him of spying.

"I stopped by for a quiet drink, forgetting it was Saturday night," he returned evenly. "I was on my way out when I happened to see the two of you."

"Don't let us stop you," she returned sarcastically.

Rolt laughed and pulled up an empty chair to sit down at their table, uninvited. "Sometimes I think you don't like me, Alanna."

"Only sometimes?" The taunt was drawn through clenched teeth.

"Yes, only sometimes," he agreed lazily. His gaze drifted suggestively to her mouth, almost physically touching it to remind her of the kisses he had stolen.

Alanna crimsoned. Somehow he made her feel as if her resistance had only been a token thing. Added to that was the sensation of guilt for failing to tell Kurt of that one visit. An arm circled her shoulders and for an instant she tensed, recalling another strong arm that had trapped her in its vice grip. She had to force herself to relax against Kurt's reassuring touch.

"The way I've been monopolizing Alanna's time lately," Kurt spoke, "hasn't given you much of a chance to compete for her, Rolt. I hate to tell you this, older brother, but you're too late now." His arm tightened around her shoulder, drawing her closer. Then he pressed a kiss on her temple. "In the not too distant future, Alanna is going to be a member of the family, all legal and binding."

His statement brought a brief surge of confidence. Alanna veiled the glitter of triumph with her lashes as she glanced swiftly at Rolt to see his reaction to Kurt's announcement. The long look he gave her was hooded and unreadable. He seemed neither surprised nor upset by the news.

The acknowledging tip of his head seemed to indicate resignation. "That's something I can drink to," Rolt smiled crookedly. "Waitress?" he turned, signaling to the girl passing their table with a tray of drinks. "A scotch and water for me, please, and two more of the same for them."

"There's one thing about my big brother," Kurt told Alanna. "Once he knows he's beaten, he admits it. Of course, he loses so seldom that he can afford to be gracious in defeat."

Yet Alanna didn't trust Rolt. She hoped that what Kurt said was true, but she couldn't forget the positive way Rolt had declared she belonged to him. When the drinks arrived, she fingered her cold glass and eyed Rolt warily.

He lifted his glass and touched it first to Kurt's, then held it against Alanna's. His enigmatic gaze held hers, not allowing her to look away.

"To the day—" his voice was firm and strong "—when Alanna becomes Mrs. Matthews."

A cold knife plunged into her heart. In that frozen moment, she knew that he meant Mrs. Rolt Matthews. He had not acknowledged defeat. What's more, Rolt was aware that she knew it even if his brother didn't. It was there in the mocking glint of his eye.

"Drink up, Alanna," Kurt prompted. His hand covered her paralyzed fingers holding the glass and carried it to her lips. The drink was in her mouth before she could stop him.

"Now that I've toasted the future bride, do you object if I dance with her?" Rolt inquired.

"Not at all." Kurt removed his arm from around her shoulders, magnanimously releasing her into his brother's custody.

Don't you see what he's doing? Alanna screamed silently at Kurt. But he merely smiled into her pale face and prodded her in the direction of his older brother, now standing expectantly beside her chair. Feeling abandoned, she rose, frozenly accepting the guiding hand on her back.

The small dance floor was crowded, as was all of the bar. Yet Alanna managed to hold herself stiffly away when Rolt turned her into his arms to begin the slow step to the music. Her fingers were rigid in his hand and her other hand rested on only a small square of his muscular shoulder. She looked sideways at the other couples rather than at her partner.

"All your maneuvering won't work, you know," she murmured beneath her breath. "I do love Kurt and I'm going to marry him."

"Are you?" he countered smoothly.

Alanna flashed him a seething look and clamped her lips tightly shut. It would be a waste of breath to try to convince him—he was too arrogant and conceited to listen. She lapsed into a frigid silence.

"How are your parents?" Rolt asked.

"Fine," she answered icily.

"Are they?" His murmuring voice was filled with knowing doubt.

Alanna missed a step and his arm immediately tightened around her waist. It wasn't a desire for small talk that had prompted his inquiry about her parents. She knew it as surely as she knew her name.

"Why do you say that?" she asked warily.

"I thought your father seemed upset about something when I was there for dinner the other evening." Rolt shrugged in seeming indifference. "Doesn't he approve of Kurt?"

How she hated the complacent glitter in those dark blue eyes! "He thinks very highly of him." Mostly because Kurt was his brother, but Alanna wouldn't admit that to Rolt even on pain of death.

"Do you know what's bothering him?"

"He's concerned about mother," she stated briskly, having no desire to discuss it with him.

"Did he tell you that?"

"Yes, he did."

The crowded dance floor had elbows and shoulders constantly pushing against her, disminishing the precious inches that kept her apart from Rolt. With the loss of each inch, his arm tightened to keep her from regaining it. His muscular thighs were now brushing against her, but her mind was too occupied with the puzzling reasons for his questions to dwell on that.

"Why are you asking all these questions about my parents?" she challenged.

"I was just curious about why your father seemed upset. Of course, if he told you that he was concerned about your mother, then I'm sure that that must be the reason." His answer was too smooth.

Her breathing became shallow. A tightness gripped her throat. "What do you know that I don't?" she demanded.

Rolt tipped his head to the side. "What makes you think I do?"

"You do know something," she declared with angry certainty. "What is it? I have a right to know."

"I'm sure you do," he agreed.

"Then tell me."

"This is hardly the place for a private discussion." His gaze arced around them.

"I want to know," repeated Alanna.

Rolt stopped and she realized the music had ended. "All right," he conceded, "I'll tell you." He paused, his gaze running over her upturned face, his expression masked and unreadable. "Come to my office on Tuesday evening at six. I'll tell the guard at the gate to expect you."

"Tuesday?" She breathed a frowning protest.

"I'm leaving in the morning. I'll be out of town until then."

Her hands doubled into fists of frustration. "This is all a trick, isn't it?" she accused. "You're making all this up just to get me to meet you."

"The only way you can be positive of that is to meet me Tuesday and find out." The line of his mouth quirked in a mirthless smile. "Shall we go back to the table before Kurt gets impatient?"

Alanna pivoted sharply on her heel. He was deliberately being mysterious. She knew that no amount of anger or pleading would make Rolt tell her anything now. If there was even anything to tell. She wasn't convinced there was, but by the same token, she wasn't convinced there wasn't.

Although Rolt left almost as soon as they returned to the table, his brief appearance ruined the rest of Alanna's evening. She couldn't recapture that mood of contentment and happiness that had accompanied Kurt's avowal of love for her. She tried to respond with the same degree of sincerity, but she knew she was faking it, although she didn't think Kurt noticed it. Her mind was torn in two by concern for her parents' well-being and the knowledge that Rolt was still intent on making her his.

The waiting added to her conflict. She didn't know if Rolt knew something about her parents or if he was pretending that he did in order to get her to agree to meet him. But if it was the latter, what difference would that make? Just because she met him it didn't mean she was suddenly going to change her mind about him. So she had to concede that there was a very real possibility that Rolt did know something.

Twice during the intervening days she cornered her father and questioned him to glean any information that might give her a clue. His answers weren't any help. The conversations left her with the impression that his problem, according to him, was that he was tired, had a sore shoulder from playing golf, and was concerned about her mother. On the surface, they seemed satisfactory, but Rolt had made her suspicious.

Alanna frowned and tugged impatiently at the stubborn weed growing in the iris bed. She didn't want to meet Rolt tonight, but it seemed the only way to put an end to all her doubts and questions. The June sun was hot. Perspiration trickled between her shoulder blades before being absorbed by the back-strap of her halter.

A car pulled into the driveway. Alanna paused to glance over her shoulder, rubbing the back of her gloved hand across her forehead. A sigh broke unexpectedly from her lips at the sight of Kurt stepping out of the car. It was not the reaction she should have had to the surprise visit from her prospective fiancé. Immediately she curved her lips into a warm smile of greeting as she straightened.

"Kurt, this is a surprise!" she declared.

"Talk about surprises," he laughed, his gaze running admiringly over her. "Somehow when I pictured Little Miss Mary working in her garden, I always saw her in ruffles and pinafores, not sexy shorts and top. I should visit her garden more often." His hands circled her waist and he kissed her soundly.

"Mmm," she sighed when he finally let her breathe again. "Now I understand why she was so contrary. She was constantly being accosted by handsome men." His hands were still locked behind her back, holding her close to him. Alanna tipped her head back to gaze into his face. "Seriously, Kurt, how did you manage to get away from the plant in the middle of the day?"

"I had an errand to run, so I took a late lunch hour," he explained.

"And you just happened to be in the area and thought you would stop, is that it?" she asked, smiling.

The teasing laughter left his eyes as he unlocked his hands. "I came to complete the last of my errand," Kurt told her. "I stopped by the jewelers and picked this up."

He took a ring box from his pocket and opened it. "It's beautiful!" breathed Alanna. She gazed at the ring, one large diamond surrounded by a circlet of smaller ones in the shape of petals.

"To make it official, Alanna, will you marry me?" he asked softly.

"Yes." Her answer was almost inaudible. The ring somehow made it all seem so much more real and unchangeable.

"Let me have your hand," said Kurt, removing the ring from its velvet holder.

Alanna raised her left hand, hastily peeling the cotton glove off, and held it out to him. Reverently he slipped it on to her finger.

"I'm afraid it's too loose," he said with a sighing grimace.

"It doesn't matter," she protested, not wanting to lose her talisman. She felt it would protect her and she didn't want to think about from what.

"Yes, it does. I want it to be perfect—as perfect as you are, Alanna," he declared huskily.

"I'm not perfect," she denied.

"To me, you are." He slipped the ring from her finger, replacing it in the box. "The jeweler said he could easily size it. I'll take it back to him this afternoon and pick it up after work tonight. And the next time I put it on your finger, it won't come off."

"No." Alanna shook her head, gazing forlornly at the box until it was out of sight once more in his pocket.

He crooked his forefinger under her chin and raised it. "We'll do it up right tonight. Champagne, candlelight, the works," he promised. "A real celebration."

Her teeth sunk whitely into her lower lip. "I can't, not tonight, Kurt," she murmured.

"Why not?" He tipped his head to the side, trying to read the expression she veiled with her lashes.

Alanna couldn't find the words to tell him she was meeting Rolf or the explanation such an announcement would require. "It's a family thing." She seized on a half-truth since the only reason she was meeting Rolf was because of his insinuations that he knew something about her parents. "If I could, I'd break it, but—"

"That's okay," he interrupted. "We'll celebrate tomorrow night."

"Yes," she agreed, relieved that he didn't press her for a more definite explanation.

"I suppose I'd better get back to work before

brother Rolt sends out a search party," Kurt sighed reluctantly.

"He is back, then, from out of town," Alanna commented.

"He got back just before noon, which is part of the reason for my late lunch break." He bent his head and kissed her. "Till tomorrow night."

Alanna waved to him as he reversed his car out of the driveway. Her interest in the garden had vanished, and her spirits were ridiculously low as she turned toward the house. She blamed it on Rolt. Just the mention of his name succeeded in spoiling her pleasure.

As she entered the house, her mother was just going up the stairs. She paused. "Was that Kurt I saw drive in?"

"Yes, it was." Alanna ran a nervous hand through her tawny hair.

"Isn't he working today?" Elinore Powell asked curiously.

"He was on his lunch break."

"Was it important? I mean, he usually doesn't come by during the day," her mother said, explaining her curiosity.

Alanna walked toward the living room. "He had an errand to run and stopped to say hello."

"I see. I'm going upstairs now to lie down for a little while, dear."

"All right, mother," she acknowledged.

As her mother disappeared up the staircase, Alanna

suddenly felt slightly sick. Why hadn't she told her
mother about the engagement ring? For that matter,
why hadn't she mentioned the engagement before
now?

It wasn't as if she was afraid her parents wouldn't
approve of her choice. They liked Kurt. She had
known since Saturday night that he wanted to marry
her. Why hadn't she told them, or at least hinted
about it? She should be deliriously happy at this moment instead of fighting waves of nausea. Why wasn't
she?

It would be all right, she assured herself. Everything would be as it should be just as soon as she had
that dreaded meeting with Rolt tonight. She was letting it worry her unnecessarily.

CHAPTER FIVE

Slowing the car, Alanna turned it into the plant entrance which was blocked by steel gates. A security guard stepped forward as she stopped. There were nervous tremors in her hands, and she clutched the steering wheel to hide them.

The guard bent down to peer through the opened car window. "Can I help you, miss?"

"Yes, I'm Miss Powell. Mr. Matthews is expecting me," she answered with a stiff smile.

The man paused to check his clipboard and nodded confirmation. "Mr. Rolt Matthews is expecting you." After clarifying to his own satisfaction which Matthews she was seeing, he signaled a second guard to open the gate and waved Alanna through.

Her face was warm as she drove in. She guessed that there were a great many workers, in high and low positions, who were familiar with the fact that she was dating Kurt steadily. Her appointment to see his brother was something that would not go unnoticed. She wished she had mentioned it to Kurt. She made a promise to herself to do it tomorrow evening before the gossip reached him and made her meeting with

Rolt sound like an assignation. Parking her car in the empty space beside the black Mark V, Alanna picked up her bag from the seat and stepped out.

She hesitated outside the car, staring at the building door. Her fears that she was on a fool's errand returned. The impulse was there to leave without seeing Rolt, but she would never be certain whether he knew anything or not if she did.

Her legs felt weak as she walked to the door. Fleetingly she regretted not eating dinner with her parents before coming, but it would have made her late. Considering the state of her nerves, the food would have probably been an uncomfortable ball in her stomach instead of providing her the strength she felt had deserted her at this moment.

Inside the building, her footsteps echoed hollowly in the empty hall leading to Rolt's office. She caught a glimpse of her reflection in a glass partition. The dusty rose of her slightly flared skirt ended at the knees, showing off the shapely curve of her calves. The silk print of the complementing blouse clung to her breasts as it tapered to her slender waist. A scarf of the same dusty rose shade as her skirt was around her throat.

She made an attractive picture, the color setting off the blond of her hair. She wished she hadn't taken such pains with her appearance. She didn't want to appear attractive for Rolt; she would rather have looked like some nonentity. It was too late to think of that now. She walked through his secretary's office to the interconnecting door. Her hand clenched once, nervously, then she knocked.

"Come in," was the muffled response.

Her stomach fluttered as she opened the door. Rolt was sitting at his desk, his head bent in an attitude of concentration over the papers spread before him. Alanna closed the door and waited just inside the room for him to acknowledge her presence.

At the click of the door, he glanced up absently, then almost immediately the indigo darkness of his eyes narrowed for a piercing second. Her heartbeat quickened under the penetrating look. Then his gaze moved to the watch gleaming goldly on his arm, as if confirming the time.

"Take a seat." He was already bending over the papers again as he spoke. "I'll be through here in a few minutes."

Alanna hesitated. A white-hot urge rose to walk over to his table and scatter his precious papers to the floor and demand that he tell her whatever it was that he was supposed to know. She had waited three days for this moment. Surely that was long enough!

No, her common sense told her. Losing her temper would only give Rolt an added advantage. This meeting was going to be strictly formal and polite. They would discuss the subject and not go into the personalities involved, his or hers. Cooling the brief surge of anger, she walked toward the half-circle of the sofa.

"There's a bar on the far wall. Ice is in the refrigerator below. Help yourself," Rolt told her.

Alanna glanced at the bar briefly and sat down on the sofa. "No, thank you." The last thing she needed was to have her thinking muddled with alcohol.

Instead she reached into her bag for a cigarette, an occasional habit she had acquired at college and one she was trying to break. But, at that moment, she was more interested in the possibly soothing effect of the nicotine on her taut nerves, especially now that her interminable wait was being lengthened still more.

Leaning against the sofa back, she exhaled a thin trail of smoke. The silence in the room was unnerving, broken only by the rustle of papers from the desk and the occasional scratch of a pen on paper. Rolt worked on, completely ignoring her presence in the room—something Alanna couldn't do as she openly gazed at him.

His expression was closed, uncompromising. He concentrated on his task and let nothing interfere. The blue drapes at the window were not completely closed. The shaft of sunlight from the window streamed over the desk, casting a golden hue on the camel tan suit he wore and shimmering over the silk of his brown tie. The angle of light brought out the amber sheen of his coffee-brown hair.

The sunlight wavered as if a filmy cloud was drifting in the way of its source. It intensified the tan of his skin until it appeared bronze, a marked contrast to the white of his shirt. The uncertain light, hovering between bright and dim, highlighted the craggy planes and angles of his masculine features. The impression Alanna had was of something savage and noble, inherently male and proud. The cloud passed and the light was steadily bright. His features again became uncompromising and closed.

She had forgotten her cigarette during her unobserved study of him, and the ash was threatening to fall as she quickly leaned toward the ashtray on the large coffee table in front of the sofa. When she straightened. Rolt was watching her, his gaze alert and inspecting. There was a mirthless curve to the molded line of his mouth. He laid the pen down with an air of finality and rose from the straight-backed chair.

"Sorry to have kept you waiting." His words were without genuine meaning, phrased in politeness and lacking in sincere apology.

"Of course," Alanna answered coolly.

Strong fingers closed around the knot of his tie, loosening it and starting to pull it free. "Do you mind?" Rolt paused.

She doubted that it really mattered to him if she gave her permission, but she did. "Not at all."

The tie was removed and stuffed in his jacket pocket. The camel tan jacket he negligently shrugged off and draped over the chair he had vacated. Alanna was gripped by the sensation that she was watching him shed the trappings of civilization. He became primitively male and somehow dangerous.

When the top three buttons of his white shirt were unfastened, he stopped. Alanna felt faintly surprised.

She had nearly expected him to strip away the shirt as well. Her senses had stirred alarmingly during those electric seconds and she looked away to bring them under control.

Instead of walking to the sofa, Rolt moved to the window, stopping in the slit of sunlight. He gazed out the dusty panes, his feet slightly apart, a stance that suggested arrogance and power. *A giant looking over his domain,* Alanna thought. Her impatience grew as he remained silent.

"What is it you claim to know about my parents?" she challenged finally.

Rolt sent a long, measuring look over his shoulder, then pivoted. "I'm going to have a drink. Are you sure you wouldn't like one?" he asked, calmly ignoring her question.

"I'm positive." It was difficult to keep the irritation she felt out of her voice.

Alanna leaned forward to crush her cigarette out in the ashtray. The bar was on the wall behind her. She listened to the opening of the refrigerator door, the clink of ice in a glass, and the closing of the door. Then there was only silence. She clasped her hands tightly together in her lap, refusing to glance around at him.

"My parents," she prompted icily.

Liquor splashed over ice. "What about them?"

"That's what I want to know." Alanna turned on the sofa cushion, glaring at Rolt. "This is a trick, isn't it? You used my parents as an excuse to lure me here, didn't you?" she accused.

He met her look with bland unconcern. "Yes."

"I should have known," she muttered. With jerky, angry movements, she grasped her bag and rose from the sofa. "You know absolutely nothing about my parents."

A half step toward the door and his quiet voice stopped her. "I didn't say that." Alanna turned to eye him warily. "I only admitted that I used them to get you here. Which is not the same as admitting that I know nothing."

"Well, do you?" she challenged, tired of the cat and mouse game.

"Sit down, Alanna." Rolt walked from the bar, a stubby glass in his hand.

"No," she refused unequivocally. "I want to know about my parents and I want to know now." There was an unmistakable threat in her voice.

His mouth twitched as though he found her barely suppressed anger amusing, but it was a fleeting movement. He walked away from the sofa, and sauntered back to his desk.

"You said your father told you that he was concerned about your mother. She has a bad heart, I believe." He paused in front of the table to glance at Alanna.

"Yes." She volunteered no more than that.

"Indirectly it's the reason why he's worried."

Alanna tipped her head to one side, definitely skeptical.

"What is the direct cause?" she asked.

"How familiar are you with your father's financial situation?" countered Rolt.

"I know they're quite comfortably fixed," she said with a haughty coolness. "Between the sale of his stock to your company and the remainder he kept, their future is adequately provided for."

"It was at the time of the sale."

That statement drifted in the air before its impact finally settled on Alanna. The haughtiness left as she searched the bronze mask. She was motionless as she tried to read between the lines. His implication sent shivers of apprehension down her spine. Slowly she began walking toward him.

"What are you saying?" The demand was breathy, lacking in strength.

"Your father never was a very good businessman or manager. Part of the money from the stock sale he invested in some solid securities. The rest went into some speculative stocks. Unfortunately they were unwise choices and he lost. Trying to recoup his losses, he cashed in the others and invested the proceeds in more risky issues. They were no more successful than the first. To put it simply, Alanna—" Rolt paused for effect "—there's no money from the stock sale."

"Oh, no, poor daddy!" she murmured to herself. Lifting her gaze, she said, "He still has the income from his stock here in the taconite plant."

"Yes, he has that, but it isn't large enough to maintain his present standard of living. If your mother had another heart attack, it would probably wipe him out completely. The house is already mortgaged. And he was at the bank this past week to apply for a loan, using his stock here as collateral."

The color drained from her face. The whole dismal picture, and its horrible repercussions, began to take shape. If her father received the loan and was unable to make the payments, the stock would be taken and his only source of income as well.

"He wanted to sell the house," Alanna said in a frozen voice. "That's why he was saying all those things to mother. And she wouldn't even consider it."

"At this point, selling the house would only buy him a little time. He should have done it a year ago," Rolt stated matter-of-factly, "before he mortgaged it."

"I don't understand." Alanna brushed a bewildered hand across her forehead and eyes. "How could it have happened? Without any warning?"

"Your father had ample warning," he pointed out dryly.

"There must be something that can be done," she said desperately, then began listing solutions aloud. "We can sell the house, of course. Mother won't object once she learns the situation. We'll move somewhere smaller, cheaper. I can get a job. For that matter, daddy can probably find something. He's intelligent. He still has his health."

"He's already tried to find work, but there aren't many positions open to a man of his age. Face it,

Alanna, he's only been at the top thanks to his father. Forgetting the age factor, he simply doesn't have the experience."

"It isn't daddy's fault that he inherited the company," Alanna protested.

"And as for you working," Rolt continued, "are you suggesting that you'll support them for the rest of your life?"

She didn't hesitate. "I don't see why not. They supported me."

"What about marriage? Are you going to forgo that? Your husband might not be so understanding when you take over the responsibility for your parents' debts and their welfare. Your father owes a considerable amount."

"He'll understand." She was thinking of Kurt, strong, wonderful Kurt.

"Do you think so?" he mocked.

"Yes."

"Your plans are quixotically beautiful, but totally unworkable. You're asking your father to sell his home. To make ends meet, he would also have to give up his membership in the various clubs. The chances of his being able to find a respectable position are virtually nil. Therefore, he would have to sit at home, with nothing to do but wait for you to give him a handout. What about his pride, Alanna? It would break him and in turn it would break your mother."

Her eyes glazed amethyst-bright with unshed tears.

She bit at her lip, knowing what Rolt said was true and loath to admit it. Proud, sensitive Dorian Powell, bred to be a gentleman and the provider of his family. It would kill him to live on her charity.

Alanna turned away to hide her trembling chin. "What's your brilliant alternative?" Sarcasm trembled in her shaking voice.

"I could help."

"He wouldn't accept charity from you," she flashed tightly.

"There is a way it could be done without him ever being aware it was charity," Rolt stated quietly.

"How?" Her breath caught, hope rising.

"I could arrange for his income from the plant to be increased. If necessary, I can put him in some public relations position, a part-time thing that would supplement his income."

"Could you?" Alanna pivoted, breathing her question.

His gaze was level and unwavering, indigo dark and hooded. "Yes, I could. I will help him...if you marry me."

Alanna stiffened, motionless for a minute. "What?"

"Marry me," Rolt repeated.

"It's impossible," she declared with a violent shake of her head. "I'm already engaged to your brother. He bought me a ring today."

Rolt lifted his glass and downed the rest of his drink. "Engagements have been broken before. That's hardly an obstacle."

"I happen to love Kurt. Isn't that an obstacle?"

"Only in your mind," he dismissed it aloofly. "It certainly wouldn't be the first loveless marriage that's taken place."

"Do you actually think I'll agree to this...this blackmail?" Alanna demanded incredulously.

"I don't think you have a choice, not if you really care about your parents as much as you claim," Rolt shrugged.

"It's preposterous!" She spun away, agitated and uncertain. "Kurt will help me. We can come up with some plan where Father won't guess where the money is coming from."

"Kurt doesn't have the kind of money required at his disposal. He works for a salary, one that would have difficulty stretching to cover two households. In our family, you work your way to the top or you don't make it. It isn't handed on a silver platter at birth." He set the glass on the table, the ice clinking against the sides. "No, Alanna, Kurt can't help you. I can, but he can't."

"I'll never marry you," she vowed. "Even the thought of it makes me violently ill."

"I offered you the only other alternative you have," he pointed out.

"I can't accept that!"

"What are going to do, then? Nothing?" His voice was nearer, signaling his approach.

"I don't know." A frustrated sigh broke from her lips. She whirled to face him, her expression angry and resentful. "You could go ahead and help him with none of your impossible strings attached!"

"Out of the goodness of my heart?" Rolt murmured wryly. "I want you, Alanna, by fair means or foul."

She knew the appeal was wasted even when she said it. "Did it ever occur to you that if you helped my father without any conditions, I might be so grateful that I would change my opinion of you?"

"It occurred to me," he acknowledged. "But changing your opinion is not becoming my wife. And that's what I want. I would rather know before I helped your father how grateful you're going to be."

Alanna thought she saw a small opening. She looked away so he couldn't see what she was thinking. "But if I agree to marry you, you will help my father?"

"When you marry me, I will help your father." Rolt closed the opening with mocking emphasis.

"If my father is ruined, Rolt Matthews, it will be your fault, because you could have saved him." She didn't attempt to mask her anger now.

"No," he denied calmly. "The fault will be yours because I made the offer and you refused. I'm not to blame for what happens—you are. I barely know your father. What difference does it make to me whether he eventually finds it difficult to hold his head up among old friends? If he was my father-in-law, I might be concerned. But as a mere acquaintance, hardly."

His arrogance filled her with rage. In a lightning arc
the open palm of her hand struck at his complacently
etched features. The needle-sharp sting of contact had
barely occurred when the guilty hand was caught in
the steel vice of his fingers. The line of his jaw was
tight and ominous.

"You will marry me, Alanna. You have no
choice," he said in a deadly quiet voice.

"Let go of me!" She strained against his hold, trying to twist her hand free.

The pressure increased by scant degrees until
Alanna was drawn closer to him to escape the ensuing
pain. His strength was such that she knew he could
easily snap the slender bones of her wrist. Caution
dictated that his streak of ruthlessness was so wide he
might do it.

She stopped struggling, her breathing deep and agitated from anger and frustration. With a defiant toss
of her head, she glared her bitter dislike of him into
his face.

The roughly hewn features were very close as the
enigmatic glitter of his gaze studied her expression.
His grip on her wrists had arched her back, pressing
her hips against the hardness of his thighs. The harsh
line of his mouth thinned into a cruel smile.

"I won't let you go. In time, I think you won't want
me to." Again, that low, arrogant voice carried the
ring of prophecy.

"No!" Alanna gasped.

His mouth moved toward hers and she turned her

head away, pushing her free hand against his chest. But there was still the pain of her captured wrist to contend with and she gained a little distance. The moist warmth of his breath hotly flamed her cheeks. The frantic turning and twisting of her head succeeded in eluding his kiss until her chin was caught by iron talons.

Her lips were ground against her teeth in savage possession. Alanna resisted, fighting his assault with every ounce of her strength. More pain shot through her arm as he twisted it behind her back, arching her against his length. Her pulse thundered in her ears.

As her strength was drained by the inescapability of his embrace, her resistance became less violent. She tried to simply endure the plundering of his mouth. The involuntary submission to his kiss brought a lethal tenderness that destroyed her defenses.

Rolt took advantage of the lowered barrier, expertly parting her lips and tasting the full sweetness of her mouth. A weakness assailed her muscles, some primitive core responding to his seductive mastery. His fingers no longer bit into her chin. His hand had drifted downward to caress her shoulder.

Long and deep, he kissed her, and a languor stole through her limbs. His mouth explored her eyelids, the sweeping curve of her lashes at the corners, burning her cheek as it moved to her earlobe, and blazed an evocative trail down the soft curve of her neck. An uncontrollable shudder quivered through her—born of desire, she discovered, instead of protest, and the realization rang a bell of alarm.

With a quick wrench, she twisted herself away from the undermining caress of his lips. She stood before him, her hands pushing against his chest, an arm's length away. He held her, not attempting to eliminate the distance between them, nor allowing her to completely break away. Alanna stared into the smoldering blue of his eyes, bewildered by the response a man she disliked had aroused, and angered that it should be so.

"Confused?" Rolt questioned in soft amusement. "Didn't you think this could happen? Didn't you realize the fire of hatred could just as quickly flame into the fire of passion?"

"No," she protested.

Quiet laughter sounded in his throat. Before she could think of anything to deny the accuracy of his taunting questions, he had closed the distance and was effortlessly sweeping her off her feet and into his arms.

"Put me down!" Alanna gasped in breathless indignation.

Rolt smiled lazily. "You aren't fully convinced yet."

Oblivious to her straining attempts to be free, he carried her to the sofa. Then Alanna was sitting across his lap, the bruising ardor of his kiss once again staking ownership to her lips. Her hands pushed futilely against his chest. One accidentally slipped inside his shirt, encountering the burning heat of his skin. Fire seared through her veins at the disturbing contact, and the fragmentary resistance melted. Her will seemed to have no control over the pagan responses of her flesh.

His fingers closed around the knot of the scarf around her throat, tugged it loose and stripped it away, exposing the full length of her slender neck for his exploration. His weight pressed her backward as he investigated the ridge of her collarbone and the hollow of her throat.

The sensuous storming of her body and mind seemed without end and a traitorous part of her didn't want it to stop. A hand moved over her waist and hip in a stimulating caress. Unfastening her blouse, he slid a hand beneath the silky material.

Through the haze of erotic sensations came the remembrance of Kurt, the man she loved. She was going to marry him. What despicable kind of a woman was she to let his brother make love to her this way? It was not only her own pride and self-respect she was betraying, but Kurt as well.

As the warm touch of Rolt's mouth moved over the rounded swell of her breast, Alanna nearly lost her newly regained sense of decency and morality in the overwhelming fire of his embrace. With a last, determined effort, she rolled free of his arms and stood beside the sofa. Her shaking limbs could carry her no farther.

Rolt held her gaze with mesmerizing ease. He sat there, his legs stretched over the cushions, his back

resting against an arm of the sofa. Alanna stood above
him, yet he was in command. Leisurely his hand
reached out, curving around the back of her knee,
stroking the sensitive skin absently. A jolting quiver
of awareness trembled through her.

"Please, don't do this, Rolt," Alanna whispered,
completely unnerved by the overpowering physical attraction he held for her.

Fluidly swinging his feet to the floor, Rolt straightened, his hand gliding upward, briefly catching the
hem of her skirt to reveal the initial curve of her thigh
before the material folds hung straight once more.
When he towered above her, the hand rested on her
waist. Her nerve ends throbbed at his closeness. She
pivoted sharply, knowing she must get away.

But his hands gripped her waist, drawing her
shoulders against his chest. He buried his face in the
soft tawny curls about her neck. Alanna closed her
eyes against the heady wine of desire. His hands slid
across her stomach, molding her against the hardness
of his frame. Her fingers pushed weakly at his hands.

"No," she protested huskily. "This is crazy. It's
only a physical...an animal attraction.

"But isn't it better, Alanna," he murmured against
the sensitive cord in her neck, "to know that when
we're married, you won't be revolted by my touch?"

"It isn't enough," she breathed, feeling herself being swamped again by his storm, and knowing a marriage couldn't be built on lust alone.

"To start with, it is." Rolt nibbled at her ear when

she twisted her neck away from the disturbing exploration of his mouth. "We'll have children and gradually a genuine fondness will grow between us."

"I don't know," Alanna sighed in confusion. She couldn't think straight, not when he was holding and caressing her the way he was.

"Believe me," he commanded.

Exerting the slightest pressure, he turned her into his arms. Like a feather caught in a whirling wind, Alanna had not the ability to dictate her own direction. She let herself be drawn into the vortex of his deepening kiss, her hands clinging to his hard shoulders to keep some measure of equilibrium.

When he finally lifted his head, she could see the light of victory glittering in his eyes. Not by word but by deed, she had involuntarily given him the answer he wanted.

But it wasn't the answer she meant to give. She didn't want to marry him. He had forced her to choose between her father and Kurt. She wanted to take back her responses to Rolt's kisses. She didn't want to choose. She wanted them both—it wasn't too late. She could change her mind—it was a woman's prerogative.

Wrenching her gaze away from his, she broke free of his loose hold and stepped past him. She squared her shoulders, preparing in her mind the words she would speak to deny again that she would marry Rolt.

As she lifted her head, she stared directly into Kurt's face, cold with contempt. Paralyzed by the sight of him standing in the opened doorway, she was barely aware of Rolt coming to her side and sliding a supporting arm around her waist.

Kurt's gaze raked her from head to foot, lingering on the gaping front of her blouse. Instinctively her hand reached up to cover it, a fiery warmth of shame burning her cheeks. It wasn't the only part of her disheveled appearance that bore signs of Rolt's lovemaking. She wanted to curl up in a little ball and die.

"I'm sorry you had to find out this way, Kurt," Rolt said quietly. "Alanna didn't know how to tell you, I guess."

Kurt's condemning gaze didn't waver from her face. "A family thing, you said." He bitterly reminded her of the reason she had given for being unable to see him tonight. "I never guessed you meant *my* family."

"Kurt, please." Alanna swallowed back a sob. "I—"

He broke in, not allowing her to finish. "I would have understood if you'd told me you were seeing Rolt. I would have been jealous as hell, but I would have understood."

"I wanted to tell you," she protested.

"But you wanted to be sure you had Rolt hooked first, is that it?" he jeered. "Why settle for the poor younger brother if you could have the rich older brother? Did you agree to marry me to force Rolt into making a similar proposal if he really wanted you as much as he claimed? Was it only an affair that he wanted in the beginning?''

"Stop it!" she cried. His poisonous arrows were inaccurate, but it didn't lessen the venom in his tone.

A chilling sound of contempt came from his throat. "Tell me, older brother—" Kurt's gaze slashed to Rolt "—are congratulations in order, or should I say condolences?''

"I've asked Alanna to marry me," Rolt admitted.

Alanna breathed in sharply. "Don't you see he's maneuvering us again, Kurt?''

"You weren't exactly unwilling, Alanna, not when I opened the door. I doubt if you ever were," he accused tightly. "And to think I believed you when you said you would show Rolt the door. You did, all right—the door to your bedroom!''

"That's not true!" Her voice lacked conviction because she guessed that Kurt must have witnessed at least part of that last kiss if not more.

"If you haven't gotten around to buying the lady—" sarcasm underlined the word "—a ring, I have one for sale cheap. It's been tried on once and guaranteed to fit. There's no sense both of us wasting our money on the same broad!''

Alanna flinched visibly at the bitter scorn in his voice. Acid tears burned her eyes, but she had no right to cry. She knew that she deserved part of Kurt's obvious disgust. "Don't Kurt, please," she murmured in a trembling voice.

"I'll leave." His mouth twisted sardonically, his

handsome features suddenly bearing a stronger resemblance to Rolt's bluntly chiseled lines. "I can guess how anxious you must be to go back into your lover's arms."

His gaze slid pointedly to the masculine hand resting possessively on the curve of her waist. Alanna hadn't been conscious of its silent support until that moment. As she moved forward to elude it, Kurt turned to leave.

"No, Kurt, wait!" She hurried after him. "Let me explain, please!"

He stopped, turning slightly. The icy disdain in his blue eyes checked the hand she held extended to touch him, freezing it in mid-air.

"Explain what?" he demanded coldly. "That you're a liar and a cheat? I know that already! I only hope that my brother is aware of what a two-timing witch you are!"

Alanna recoiled as if he had slapped her. The words died in her throat. She stared at the floor, listening to Kurt's footsteps as he walked away. When not even their echo could be heard, she turned. She felt frozen and knew it was shock that numbed her.

Rolt was still standing beside the sofa. His alert gaze was watching her, yet not betraying a flicker of his thoughts. She lifted her chin a fraction, wide, pain-filled eyes meeting his look.

"You arranged for Kurt to come here tonight, didn't you?" she accused in an emotionless voice.

"Yes."

"Why?" There was a slight break in her bland voice.

"I thought it would be the best way for him to find out you were going to marry me. It was a harsh way, but the best way in the end," Rolt said with remarkable unconcern.

"I'm going to marry you," she said. "You've succeeded in that goal." She walked to him, standing motionless as he gazed down at her.

"I'll keep my word about helping your father."

"You'd better savor this moment," Alanna warned him coldly. "You have what you want, but I don't think you'll want it once it's really yours."

His brow flicked upward. "Which means?" he prompted dryly.

"Which means that I intend to make your life as miserable as you've made mine," she stated. "I will marry you, Rolt, but I'll make you pay for the rest of your life for what you did here tonight. You'll regret making me your wife."

Rolt looked at her for a long moment, then turned away. He didn't seem at all concerned about her prediction. "Get your bag. It's time we informed your parents of the glad tidings."

CHAPTER SIX

THE BLACK MARK V followed Alanna's car like an ominous, dark shadow, Alanna wouldn't let herself think about what she'd done. There would be time enough for regrets and self-recrimination later. With her mind blank, mechanical reflexes guided her car into the driveway. Rolt was only seconds behind her.

Alanna stood beside her car, waiting for him to join her before entering the house. As he walked toward her with effortless, long strides, his forcefully masculine features were thrown into sharp relief by the angle of light from the setting sun.

Suddenly she could feel the hard length of his body molded against hers and the betraying clamoring of her senses in response. With a brief shake of her head, she chased the unnerving sensation away. This physical attraction was the one thing she must guard against at all costs.

"Shall we go in?" She anticipated an affirmative answer to her stiff inquiry and turned toward the house.

"In a minute." His had gripped her elbow to detain her, but immediately she jerked it free. "That's something you can't do when we're inside, Alanna," Rolt reminded her mockingly. "We're supposed to be madly in love. Isn't that what you want your parents to believe?"

"We're not inside yet," she said icily, and started again toward the house.

This time he didn't detain her, but followed a step behind. When his arm reached around her for the doorknob, Alanna paused, waiting for him to open the door. Instead she found herself suddenly trapped between Rolt and the door. Her head jerked upward to remind him scathingly that they were not in the house, but the words never had a chance to leave her lips.

With the graceful and deadly accurate swoop of an eagle, his mouth closed over hers. For a fleeting second Alanna was immobilized by searing surprise. When she would have twisted away from his hard kiss, he was already releasing her. She was so angry at herself for being caught unaware—and at him for taking advantage of it—that she couldn't speak.

The door opened under his hand. "We can go in now." He smiled arrogantly down at her and added, "Now that there's a sparkle in your eye and a rather becoming blush to your cheeks. We can't be meeting your parents with you looking as if you've agreed to marry the hangman."

"It's much worse. I'm going to marry you," she hissed.

The taunting softness of his laughter heightened

the pink in her cheeks as he followed her into the house. Knowing he was right didn't ease her anger. She must put on an act for her parents. She didn't want them suspecting that she had any motive other than love for marrying Rolt.

As they entered the living room, her father folded up the evening paper and rose to meet them, slipping his reading glasses into his shirt pocket.

"Hello, Rolt. Elinore said she thought it was your car that drove in behind Alanna," her father said with a smile of welcome. "Is it business or pleasure, I hope, that brings you here tonight?"

When the flat of his hand spread over the small of her back, Alanna couldn't help starting. Her gaze flew to his face, bright with resentment, telling him she would endure his touch but she didn't like it. Her heart turned over at the unbelievable warmth shining in his eyes that were regarding her so softly. She simply couldn't look away.

Careful, a voice warned, *don't be taken in by his charm. Remember why you agreed to marry him. When you bring Rolt down, make certain you don't topple as well.*

It was with an effort that she tore her gaze away from Rolt. A self-conscious light entered her violet eyes as she encountered the curious and puzzled expression of her father. She glanced swiftly at her mother sitting on the couch. Elinore Powell was eyeing the two of them with an expectant gleam.

"Tonight your daughter consented to be my wife,"

Rolt announced quietly. His gaze finally left her face to look at her father. "With your permission, of course."

The tacked-on phrase was a polite gesture. Alanna knew Rolt didn't care whether her parents approved of their marriage or not. And she knew she would marry him with or without their permission.

Dorian Powell was momentarily stunned by the news, but not her mother. She rose from the couch, her face wreathed in a smile as she hurried to embrace Alanna.

"I'm so happy for you, darling," she exclaimed in a voice trembling with emotion. Tears of happiness shimmered in her eyes. "You didn't fool me for a minute. I knew it all the time, didn't I?"

"Yes, mother," Alanna acknowledged, her gaze unwillingly sliding to meet Rolt's narrowed, questioning look.

"You knew it all the time, Mrs. Powell?" he smiled. His head was tipped curiously to one side, but Alanna noted the piercing sharpness of his eyes.

"Yes." Her mother stepped back, holding on to Alanna's hands as she smiled happily from one to the other. "Call it a mother's instinct or female intuition, but I just knew all along that Alanna was in love with you."

"You might have said something to me." Dorian Powell laughed with still a trace of bewilderment at the unexpected turn of events. "I am her father, you know."

"You would have accused me of being silly and sentimental if I had," her mother declared. "It was just that Alanna reminded me so much of myself. Remember how infuriated and angry I was, Dorian, when you first started coming to call. It didn't last long, though."

The dancing light in Rolt's eyes raised Alanna's temperature. She had to keep silent because of her parents, but she let her gaze tell him that she despised him heartily and for ever.

"I remember," her father chuckled. "For such a petite thing, you had a man-sized temper and I felt the force of it many times. Alanna is like her mother in many ways."

Rolt's hand slid to the curve of her waist and drew her length against his side. Her fingers curled over his hand, unobtrusively trying to loosen his hold.

"Daddy, you're going to have Rolt thinking he's marrying a shrew with all this talk about temper and being angry," she scolded with a forced laugh.

"You mean, I'm not?" Rolt laughed near her ear.

She would have loved to scratch his eyes out at that moment. He was enjoying this situation tremendously and all at her expense.

"Of course she isn't," her father rejoined with a loving smile at his daughter. "I must say, Rolt, I really thought if I was going to be giving Alanna away in marriage to anyone in the near future, it would be Kurt. This has taken me completely by surprise. But, believe, me, I couldn't be happier with her choice."

"Thank you, Dorian. Neither could I." Rolt again treated her to one of those adoring looks that was underlined with mockery.

"Kurt," her mother murmured in sudden remorse. "Poor Kurt. He was so very fond of you, Alanna."

"Yes, mother, I know." The pain in her voice was genuine.

"I do hope he isn't bitter. He does know, doesn't he?" Elinore frowned.

Alanna couldn't answer the question. The mention of Kurt brought too much anger to her tongue. She closed her lips tightly to keep the rush of vindictive words from pouring out. Rolt had destroyed Kurt's happiness and her own to get what he wanted.

"We saw him tonight," Rolt answered, not explaining the circumstances.

"It was difficult for all of us, but I know it will work out for the best."

"Yes," her mother agreed. "It would have been simply terrible if Alanna had married Kurt, then discovered she really loved you. Kurt might be hurt in the beginning, but he'll get over it."

"Yes, yes," her father nodded. "A little pain now is better than a lot of pain later." Sensitive as he always was, he recognized that the conversation made Alanna uncomfortable without knowing the true reason. "But there isn't any need to discuss that. Why don't we sit down? Elinore, maybe you could check to see if there's any coffee left and some of that delicious cake Ruth made. And tell Ruth the news, too."

"I certainly will," Elinore Powell agreed enthusiastically. "At least Alanna has finally started the process that will bring us our future grandchildren."

"In due course, my dear," Dorian Powell laughed. "In due course."

Children. Color mounted in Alanna's cheeks at the ultimate intimacy the thought implied. With the firm, masculine hand around her waist, her senses leaped in response, and she moved quickly away from the hand toward the sofa. She must stop these sensual longings. It was imperative that she never indulge in them with Rolt.

She had barely sat down on the sofa when Rolt was beside her. He didn't exactly sit close, but his arm was draped along the back to let his hand rest lightly on her shoulder. A small liberty, but she slid him a resentful glance from beneath her lashes just the same.

Her father turned to them as her mother left the room. "Elinore has her heart set on grandchildren," he said affectionately and with a hint of apology. "She always wanted a houseful of children, but unfortunately she wasn't able to have them. We consider ourselves blessed that we have you, Alanna. So don't you be worried about disappointing your mother if you decide you and Rolt want to wait before starting a family."

"Actually, dad, Rolt and I haven't talked about that," she said nervously. "I don't know if he likes children."

"I like children," he told her, smiling lazily. "Especially little girls with dark amber hair and beautiful violet blue eyes."

Desperately she wanted the subject changed. And she wanted his hand off her shoulder. The absent rubbing caress of his fingers made her feel weakly vulnerable, especially combined with the topic of conversation, and she steeled herself to ignore it. She disliked him intensely. She hated him!

The tall, spare housekeeper swept into the room, her angular face alight with joy. Alanna could have cried with relief. Amidst the hugs, congratulations and explanations, the subject of children was lost.

"It's just like having one of my own getting married," Ruth declared. "I've known Alanna since she was a baby." Her mother entered the room with a tray of coffee and cakes, and Ruth rushed quickly to take it from her. "I told you to leave that, Elly. It's too heavy for you."

"Nonsense," her mother denied. "I only have a few feet to go anyway. You just sit back down."

Ruth did, insisting she would pour. The spout of the pot was poised above the first cup when she put it back on the tray. "Just think, Elly, of all there is to be done." She glanced at Alanna. "When is the wedding? Have you thought about a date yet?"

Alanna was about to say that they hadn't had time, but she never had a chance to speak.

"Right away," Rolt answered. "Alanna wants to be a June bride."

She wanted no such thing! She turned to glare at him and deny his statement. His fingers dug into her shoulder in warning. There had been no mention of when they would marry, but she hadn't dreamed it would be this soon. Of course, what difference did it really make? she thought bitterly.

"June!" Elinore Powell explained. "But there's less than ten days left of this month. We have to buy your gown and the bridesmaid's dresses. And the invitations, they have to be printed. And arrangements for the church and flowers. Ruth can make the cake, but—"

"I think we'd rather have a quiet wedding, Mrs. Powell," Rolt said gently.

With that, Alanna was in full agreement. A large wedding with lots of guests and a drawn-out reception seemed hypocritical. The marriage vows would be enough of a farce.

"I'm sorry, mother." She knew how much her mother had counted on a big, beautiful church wedding for her only child. "We really would rather have just a simple ceremony with only the family in attendance."

If Alanna had doubted Rolt when he told her of her father's precarious financial circumstances, it was banished. The releif on his face was visible at her statement. He would never have been able to afford the expense of a large wedding.

"If that's what you want," her mother sighed a reluctant agreement.

"In this day and age," Ruth sniffed, "you should be glad they're getting married without worrying about the size of the wedding."

"What about a honeymoon?" Elinore ignored her friend's comment.

"A long weekend is the best I can manage," Rolt stated. "We'll have to postpone it until winter."

It didn't matter, Alanna thought. The honeymoon would be over before it began. It was a relief to learn that she wouldn't be forced to spend an extended length of time exclusively in his company.

The wedding and related topics dominated the conversation for the next hour. Alanna's participation was small, letting her mother and Ruth talk over the plans and what was possible during the short time they had.

"Flowers. The flowers will have to be decided on, too," Ruth added. "What kind of flowers would you like in your wedding bouquet, Alanna?" she asked as she picked up the coffee pot to refill their cups. It was empty. "We're out of coffee. I'll go and make another pot."

"Please, none for me," Rolt forestalled, removing his arm from the back of the sofa. "It's time I was leaving."

"Not so soon," her mother protested.

"Yes," he insisted, straightening to his feet.

He said goodbye to each of them in turn and started from the room. Alanna had remained seated until she felt the expectant looks from her parents and realized they thought she would want to accompany him to the door, so they could say good-night alone. With gritted teeth, she rose quickly.

"I'll see you to the door, Rolt," she called after him.

He halted in the doorway to the hall and waited until she had joined him. "There isn't any need," he told her. His hand cupped the side of her face. "It's been a hectic evening, all things considered. Have an early night and I'll see you tomorrow."

Her hand gripped his wrist. She knew he intended to kiss her. There was nothing she could do to stop him with her parents and Ruth looking on. That was the way Rolt had planned it—the glint in his eyes told her so.

His mouth closed warmly over hers. She kept her lips cool and unresponsive. She would show him that just because she had been putty in his hands once, it wasn't going to always be true. In fact, she was determined it would never happen again.

When he lifted his head, her eyes glittered triumphantly. *How do you like kissing an ice cube?* her gaze taunted. His mouth twisted in dry amusement.

"You can do better than that," he murmured for her hearing alone. "But I'll wait for another time to prove it to you."

"You're in for a long wait," she muttered, smiling sweetly for her parents' benefit.

His thumb rubbed the corner of her mouth for a second, then he released her.

"Goodnight, darling. Sleep well."

The endearment had been a deliberate taunt. So had the wish for a good night's sleep. Neither was true. She would never be his darling and she knew she wouldn't sleep.

"Goodnight, Rolt."

It was the first of a succession of nights that Alanna had to endure. Her parents expected her to be with Rolt and she had little recourse but to see him. Although she constantly had to steel herself against his touch or an arm around her shoulders, an occasional kiss, Rolt didn't make any attempt to make love to her.

In a way, she found it strange. But she reasoned that he was trying to win her by degrees, getting her to trust him, then taking advantage of it. As far as she was concerned he had proved that he wasn't to be trusted.

Mostly Alanna didn't have much time to think about what she was doing. There was shopping to be done, a simple wedding dress and a small trousseau. Alanna insisted it be small because she knew her father could afford nothing else and because she didn't care.

THE MORNING OF HER WEDDING it was raining—sheets of water driving against the window pane of her bedroom. It seemed fitting that it should rain, she thought, as her mother helped her dress. According to superstition, a marriage was headed for trouble if it rained on the bride on her wedding day. Alanna considered it a good omen for her plans.

When she rode with her parents to the church, a shaft of sunlight pierced the dark clouds. She bit her lip tightly to keep from screaming for it to go away. It was only a silly superstition. She would never be happy married to Rolt whether the sun shone on her wedding day or not.

When she left the church on her husband's arm, the sky was clearing. Everything appeared freshly scrubbed and crystal bright, the air refreshing and clean. Alanna didn't notice the vivid green of the trees as they drove to her parents' house for the small wedding reception.

Stoically she endured the endless offers of congratulations and best wishes. She couldn't accept any of them honestly, so she simply smiled and nodded. If any of the guests noticed her quietness, they attributed it to bridal jitters. She kept smiling until she was virtually gritting her teeth to maintain the brittle pose.

At last Rolt suggested that they could leave. Alanna nodded a quick agreement, her rigid muscles relaxing briefly against the arm that had rarely left her waist. As she embraced her parents, she experienced a qualm of misgiving about what she was doing and why, but pushed it aside.

Amidst a shower of rice, she left the house with Rolt. His black car was parked in the drive. Only it wasn't solid black any more. There were white curls and stripes and slogans of *Just Married* and *His and*

Hers painted on the sides, decorations done in good fun. But Alanna didn't find them amusing. It only served to point out that she had married Rolt for revenge and not love.

"You can relax now, Alanna. It's over," Rolt said dryly after reversing the car on to the road.

"Yes." At least the need to keep up a pretense was over. With a sigh, she leaned against the seat back. "How long will it take to reach your house?"

"It's about a twenty-minute drive from here to our home," he answered with quiet emphasis.

The silence during the drive was mutually enforced. There had never been any suggestion that their wedding night would be spent anywhere but at Rolt's house. Had he suggested spending the weekend at a hotel, Alanna would have refused. A hotel room was dominated by the bed. In a house, there were other rooms.

She had never been to his house, never seen it. Her father had taken most of her things, those that weren't packed in the suitcases now in the truck of the car, to the house the day before. She knew its general direction and that it was in the country near a lake.

Tall pines overshadowed the lane leading to the house. They grew so close to the road that it was nearly like driving through a tunnel. In a clearing just below the crest of a hill stood the house. It was built of unfinished cedar, rustic and rambling, blending naturally with its forest surroundings.

Attractive, Alanna admitted, in spite of the fact that it belonged to Rolt. The car stopped and he walked around to open her door.

"My suitcases," she reminded him as he walked toward the wooden steps leading to the front door.

"I'll bring them in later." He unlocked the door and waited on the wide, rustic porch for her to join him. When she would have walked past him, his hand stopped her. "There is an old custom about carrying a bride across the threshold."

Her first impulse was to object, but she stifled it and let his strong arms cradle her against his chest. Her pulse stirred for an instant at the hard contact with his muscular shape, but she kept her grip on her icy composure. Rolt nudged the door open with his foot and carried her into the house.

"The custom has been observed. You may put me down now," Alanna said with chilling calmness.

His face was very close to hers, his gaze steady and unreadable. She could make out every detail from the faint, sun-weathered lines at the corners of his eyes to the harsh grooves carved near his mouth. For several long seconds, he held her. A peculiar tension vibrated along her taut nerves.

Slowly the arm under her knees relaxed, letting her legs slide to the carpeted floor. The other arm tightened its hold, flattening her breasts against the granite wall of his chest. She held herself rigid, neither struggling nor submitting.

Rolt tipped her chin upward.

"Welcome home, Mrs. Matthews."

His mouth descended on hers with slow insistence. Controlled passion edged the possession. Alanna blocked out the hard strength of his arms and concentrated her thoughts on Kurt, the man she should have married, the man she would have married. It helped her ignore the persuasive pressure of his kiss.

There was a tightness to the line of his jaw when he raised his head. "You're not going to try to make this easy, are you?" For all the coolness of his voice, his eyes were sapphire chips of fiery blue.

"It was never my intention to make anything easy for you," she replied.

His arm tightened for a punishing second, then let her go. She stepped smoothly away from him, aware of a faint quiver in her knees, but she had successfully repelled his kiss. She was determined it would be the first of many times.

Ignoring Rolt, she glanced about the room. Smooth, unfinished cedar paneled the walls, broken often by large windows with a fireplace of large sand-colored stone. The carpet of cream beige was a luxuriously thick, deep shag, its rough texture in keeping with the style of the home. A long sofa was in front of the fireplace, covered in a rich brown velvet, and matching love-seats flanked the sofa in a cream and brown plaid. Indirect lighting was concealed in the beamed ceiling.

An extra wide hallway allowed her a glimpse of the dining room with windows running the length of one wall. The planks and railings of a sun deck were visible through the panes. There was a movement from Rolt, who had been standing some distance behind her. Alanna turned, as if she had forgotten his presence, which was an impossibility. The look in his eyes invited a comment about the house.

"It's very nice," she said indifferently.

"I'll show you around."

Without waiting to see if she wanted to, Rolt walked past her into the wide hallway. Shrugging a disinterest that wasn't true, Alanna followed. He gestured toward an open door leading off the hall, one she hadn't noticed.

"The study, where I sometimes work in the evenings," he said, and continued into the dining room.

Alanna looked in briefly, and had the sensation of a warm, dark cave, lined with books and dark leather furniture and the same pale beige carpet.

"The dining room, and beyond it the sun deck." There was a libreral use of ochres and bronzed golds in the sun-filled room and a breathtaking view of the lake at the bottom of the hill. "The kitchen is through there." His hand waved toward a wide arch and the native wood tone of the cupboards that could partially be seen. Alanna glanced around the opening at the kitchen filled with modern appliances in a setting that was decidely homespun. She followed when Rolt returned to the hall and the open L-shaped staircase leading to the second floor.

At the top of the stairs, another wide hall encircled

the open stairwell, protected by a smoothly finished cedar railing to match the paneled walls. Three doors branched off from the hall, two on the front side of the house and one on the lake side.

"The bedrooms," stated Rolt.

"Obviously," she shrugged dryly.

"The two on the other side are the guest rooms and this is the main bedroom." He opened the door to the main bedroom as she had expected he would.

A king-size bed dominated the spacious room, a spread of shimmering brown velvet covering its vast width. Windows flanked the bed, paned squares running nearly floor to ceiling. Again there was a panoramic view of the tree-lined lake, glittering mirror-smooth in the distance.

"Very nice," Alanna commented with marked indifference.

"There's a walk-in closet behind that door." Rolt gestured toward the left. "And the private bathroom is on the right side. You can look around while I bring your suitcases up."

Alanna looked at the doors he had indicated, but didn't investigate. Nor did she make any remark about the suitcases. She didn't move until she heard Rolt at the bottom of the stairs. Then she walked into the hallway and around the stairwell to the other bedrooms. Both were small, at least by the standard of the master bedroom, and tastefully furnished. When she heard Rolt reenter the house, she walked quickly back to the master bedroom. Setting her two suitcases near

the bed, he straightened, giving her a long, level look
as if trying to measure her mood.

Aloofly she turned around to face the window,
wanting to take no chances that he might read what
was on her mind.

"If you'll excuse me—" mockery laced with cynicism was in his voice "—I'll change my clothes."

"Into something more comfortable?" she inquired
acidly.

"Exactly." His mouth quirked. "I don't generally
sit around the house in a suit and tie."

Alanna didn't move from the window as he entered
the walk-in closet. Minutes later he emerged. Her
hearbeat quickened in alarm.

"Don't worry," his voice laughed silently at her
frozen position. "It's quite safe to turn around."

With a defiant toss of her head, Alanna glanced
over her shoulder, bracing herself only to find there
was no need. Rolt was wairing a pair of brushed de-
nims and a patterned shirt of blue and brown. Amusement glittered in his eyes as he noted the relief that
flashed across her face.

"While you unpack your things, I'm going to wash
the wedding decorations off the car." Laughter lurked
at the corners of his mouth.

With a brief mocking nod, he left again. For the
second time, Alanna waited until he was at the bottom of the stairs. Then she picked up both suitcases
and carried them across the hall to one of the spare
bedrooms. Opening the suitcases, she began unpack-

ing her clothes and putting them away. The first suitcase was empty and the second one had only a few items left in it when she heard the front door open and close. She paused for several seconds, straining to hear the sounds of Rolt's footsteps on the thick carpet. She heard him on the stairs and stiffened for an instant, nibbling apprehensively at her lower lip as he reached the top.

The door to the spare room where Alanna was stood ajar. She knew that when Rolt didn't find her in the master bedroom, he would notice it. A second later he was in the hall. Quickly she busied her fingers with buttoning a blouse on a wire hanger. Although her back was to the door, and the carpet muffled his footsteps, she knew the very instant he entered the room, and prickles ran along the back of her neck.

"What are you doing in here?" As if he hadn't already guessed.

"Unpacking." Alanna made a show of making certain the blouse hung straight, the collar smooth.

"The master bedroom is across the hall," Rolt said very calmly, making it sound as if he thought she wasn't aready acquainted with the fact.

"I prefer this one," she responded airily, and walked to the closet to hang the blouse with the other clothes she had put there.

"Is that right?" he asked, his voice dry and low.

Returning to the suitcase, Alanna was forced to let her gaze at least richochet off his. His features were taut and grim, an unyielding hardness that made her think he would rip her clothes from the closet and carry them into the master bedroom. But she couldn't back down and she wouldn't.

"Do you have any objections?" She kept the air of unconcern in her voice as she took another blouse from the case and began draping it around a hanger. The tension in the air was now electrically charged.

"Plenty of objections," he responded. Then his tone visibly relaxed. "But we'll discuss them in detail later."

Pivoting, he left the room, letting his silent threat intimidate her almost as effectively as his presence had done. She sat weakly on the bed, the blouse rumpled in her lap. It hadn't been exactly a battle, just another small skirmish. She had escaped unscathed so far. She could only cross her fingers and hope that her luck would hold.

Half an hour later, her clothes were all put away and she had changed out of the simple white dress she had been married in and into a scarlet pantsuit. The wide flared legs swirled about her ankles like a long skirt. The draping neckline of the tunic-styled top accented her slender throat.

She stood in front of the mirror, idly flipping the ends of her hair with a brush. She couldn't spend the rest of the afternoon and evening in the bedroom, and there was no longer any reason to stay. With a sigh, she placed the hairbrush on the dresser top and walked into the hall. There hadn't been a sound from downstairs. She had no idea if Rolt was in the house.

At the bottom of the stairs, she saw him out on the sun deck. One foot was on the lower railing running around the edge. An elbow rested on his knee as he gazed down the hill at the lake. Alanna debated whether to join him or to wait in the living room for him to come in search of her.

She was about to decide on the living room, feeling it might not be wise to take the battle to the enemy. She still had to store up her defenses. At that moment, Rolt straightened and turned, looking directly at her, evidently able to see through the window as clearly as she could.

"The view of the lake is excellent from here," he said.

Startled at the clearness of his voice when he was outside and she was in, it took Alanna a full second to realize that the door to the sun deck was open.

She hesitated another second before walking to the door.

Rolt leaned a hip against the railing and waited. The disturbing intensity of his gaze nearly made her turn around and go back into the house. She wasn't afraid, she reminded herself, and kept walking steadily to the rail stopping two feet to his left.

The lake was what he had invited her to see, so that was what she looked at. The sun deck was elevated above the slope of the hill. There had been a careful clearing of trees from the hill to keep the view from being obstructed and still leave foliage on the hillside.

"All settled in?" came his low, amused voice.

"Very comfortable, yes," she nodded, adding coolly, "it's quite a view of the lake."

"I like it," Rolt answered simply.

"Isn't it inconvenient to live in the country, especially in winter when the roads are bad and blocked with snow?" Alanna needed to keep the conversation going. For some reason, she couldn't tolerate silence between them with this serenely beautiful view before them. She seized on the first thought that came to mind.

"Sometimes," Rolt acknowledged. "But after the noise of the plant, and the hustle, I like the peace and quiet here. No neighbors to trouble you—human neighbors that is. Just the coyote and squirrel and the loon."

No neighbors, Alanna thought, none that she could run to, whatever the reason. The thought chilled her. She was all alone out here with Rolt. She couldn't help wondering how long the sleeping giant of Mesabi would continue to sleep.

"Alanna."

She jumped at the sound of her name. She tried to conceal it by turning to face him, but she saw the flick of his eyebrow that said he had seen.

"There was something I wanted to ask you," Rolt said.

"What's that?" She brushed a stray curl from her cheek, searching her mind for any question he might want to ask and coming up blank.

"Were you planning to cook tonight's dinner or

shall I?" The impulse was to say that she wasn't very hungry. The fact was her stomach felt suddenly very empty at the mention of dinner.

"I will," she agreed, glad of something to do that would take her out of Rolt's company.

CHAPTER SEVEN

THE SUN LINGERED with infuriating stubbornness before finally sinking behind the western horizon to end the long summer day. Twilight challenged the encroaching darkness for a brief time, then fled after the sun.

Its departure was Alanna's signal to exit. With a pretense at casualness, she closed the unabsorbing magazine and tossed it negligently on the seat cushion beside her. The action attracted the blue of Rolt's gaze. They had barely exchanged a word all evening.

The threatened discussion of his objections to the sleeping arrangements hadn't taken place. Alanna guessed that he didn't intend the discussion to take place in the living room. She was certain he had another room in mind. Rising from the sofa, she flicked him a deliberately cool glance.

"Goodnight, Rolt," she said in an offhand way, and walked toward the staircase in the hall.

"Turning in so early?" His response was dry with mockery.

Alanna paused on the first step, her hand resting on the banister post. "It's been a long day," she answered diffidently.

There wasn't any wish from Rolt that she have a good night. She took note of the omission as she mounted the stairs. It served to stiffen her resolve. Inside her room, she locked the door. Then, doubting the strength of the lock, she hurried to the long dresser and began pushing it in front of the door, thankful there were wheels on the bottom.

Feeling a little more secure, she glanced around the room, her gaze stopping on the bathroom door. The two guests shared the same bath. Alanna rushed to lock that door and dragged a chair in front of it. *There*, she thought with satisfaction, *the entrances are blocked. Let Rolt try to make his objections now!*

Stripping, she changed into her nightgown and robe. It was a clinging silk-like material, ivory with an abundance of lace about the bodice, part of the trousseau her mother had insisted she buy. Alanna would have preferred her shapeless cotton gown, but wasn't about to go look for it now.

Sleep was far from her thoughts. Alanna didn't even go near the bed. She was intelligent enough to realize that her defenses weren't necessarily impregnable. If Rolt should breach them, she didn't want to be lying in bed when he entered the room.

Pacing restlessly, she waited. Her mind ran ahead, rehearsing all the vile, hateful things she would say to him—disgusting, loathsome, a contemptible beast, barbaric and cruel. Alanna would remind him in vindictive terms of the way he had blackmailed her.

If he dared come near her, she would bite and claw

at him like a wildcat. Exhilaration flamed through her
veins. She was ready to do battle. All her weapons
were at hand, ready for use. And she waited for the
opportunity, her eyes spakling, her air confident.

She waited and waited and waited. Ten-thirty, ele-
ven o'clock, eleven-thirty, and still there was no siege
at her door. From her window, she could see the
square of light shining out from the living room below. Weariness was invading her muscles. The bed
looked more and more inviting, but she resolutely remained upright. The mounting tension scraped at her
already raw nerves.

Walking to the window for what seemed the hun-
dredth time, she leaned against the frame. What was
he doing down there? Why was he waiting? For her to
grow tired and lower her defenses?

She stared into the darkness. Then, blinking in disbelief, she realized that the living room light was off.
Rolt must be coming upstairs. Spinning, she faced the
door.

Her fingers clutched the top of the robe together.
She suddenly had visions of Rolt bursting through the
door, laughing at the verbal abuse she hurled at him,
stripping the gown from her and throwing her onto
the bed. Her lips could almost feel the arousing
warmth of his mouth.

She thrust the image away. That would never happen. Rolt would not overwhelm her without first feeling the fury of her wrath. Quickly she turned off the
light, throwing the room into darkness. Let him think

she was in bed asleep. Holding her breath, she listened.

Rolt was at the top of the stairs and moving along the hall. A door opened and closed—it had to be the master bedroom. There was a series of indefinable sounds that might be made by someone getting ready for bed. Water ran briefly, then silence.

Minutes ticked by and Alanna watched the door. There was absolutely no movement from the master bedroom. Gradually she was forced to realize that Rolt had gone to bed. To bed! The silent scream of frustration exploded inside her. How dared he? This was their wedding night! He should be at her door! How could he go to bed! Alanna flung herself on the bed, beating the pillow with impotent rage.

Nearly an hour later she accepted the fact that Rolt had indeed gone to bed and crawled beneath the covers of her own. She slept fitfully, waking at the slightest night sound, till finally, near dawn, exhaustion drugged her into a heavy sleep.

Slowly, reluctantly, she awakened to a midmorning sun, momentarily confused by the unfamiliar room. Remembering where she was, she tensed, listening. There was only silence. Where was Rolt? There was a noise outside her window. Slipping from under the covers, she went to investigate.

In the drive below she could see Rolt walking toward the corner of the house. He was carrying a rod and reel and tackle box. She watched him disappear around the house in the direction of the lake. She didn't question her good fortune at being left alone, but took advantage of it instead.

The chair was moved away from the bathroom door. The procelain tub beckoned to her as she entered. A long soak would ease the aching tiredness of her muscles and help eliminate the drugged feeling of her senses. She turned on the taps and added a generous amount of the bubble bath she found on the shelf, then while the tub was filling with water, she brushed the woolly taste from her mouth and laid out the clothes she would wear on the bed.

Later, immersed up to her neck, Alanna felt deliciously indulged and pampered. Frothy bubbles peaked and mounded around her. The comfortably hot water was soothing. She rested her head against the back of the tub and closed her eyes, enjoying the sensations.

The door to the second bedroom opened. Foolishly she had forgotten to lock it. She sat up with a start and just as quickly sank below the concealing bubbles. She had forgotten about Rolt. She couldn't do that any more. He was leaning against the door frame, staring at her.

"Get out of here!" she hurled indignantly.

"Why?" The bemused glitter in his eyes betrayed the bland expression on his face.

"I'm taking a bath, that's why," Alanna retorted.

"I noticed that." The grooves near his mouth deepened slightly.

"I would like some privacy." She pressed her lips

tightly together. It wouldn't do to lose her temper when she was in such a vulnerable position.

"Does it bother you to have me watch?"

"You know it does," she hissed tautly.

"That's too bad." Rolt shrugged and folded his arms in front of him. There was an unmistakable challenge in his stance that dared her to try to throw him out. "Are you going to be in there much longer? I'm getting hungry for breakfast."

"Go and fix your own!" Alanna glared, hating him intensely for putting her in such an awkward position.

"I couldn't deprive you of the privilege," he mocked.

That did it. "Privilege!" she exploded. "You've made the man I love think I'm some cheap, money-hungry tramp, then blackmailed me, using my parents, into marrying you. And you dare to suggest that fixing a meal for you is a privilege. You are the lowest, most contemptible being on earth! You're not even a being—you're a thing!"

His eyes grew cold and hard. "You've been rehearsing that little speech for quite a while, haven't you?" Rolt taunted harshly. "Do you have any more stored up?"

"Millions!"

"Don't stop now." His lips curled in a jeer. "Let's hear them all. I have plenty of time."

Alanna couldn't decide whether the bathwater had suddenly cooled or her temperature had risen to boiling point, but her skin suddenly felt cold. She wanted to be out of the tub, with something more substantial covering her than the slowly dissipating bubbles.

"Will you get out of here?" She choked on her anger.

"Come now, my little fishwife," he taunted again. "You haven't used disgusting and loathsome yet. How about replusive? You do find me replusive, don't you?" The hard and knowing glint in his eye reminded her of that time when she had responded unrestrainedly to his caresses.

The submerged washcloth drifted close to her hand. Her fingers closed around the saturated cloth. Blinded with anger, she flung it at his head, a spray of water scattering over the tiled floor, and a few drops landed harmlessly on his bronzed features.

"Get out of here!" Her voice trembled hoarsely.

"Discounting the fact that your aim was off, you should have thrown something more deadly than a washcloth," Rolt informed her, straightening away from the door frame and moving toward her with ominous purpose.

Wildly Alanna reached for the rosettes of soap in the dish beside the bathtub. She pelted him with two of them, but the third didn't have a chance to leave her hand as her wrist was caught by the biting grip of his fingers.

"Drop it," he ordered, and twisted her hand back until the pink rosette slipped from her pain-charged fingers.

Her fingers clawed at the hand that held her wrist.

A twin grip closed around the other hand and Rolt dragged her out of the tub. Water and bubbles splashed everywhere as she tried to resist when he hauled her against his chest. The slippery tile floor offered little footing, hampering her efforts to kick at him.

Rolt twisted her arms behind her back, crushing her against his granite length, and applied pressure to his brutal hold. Alanna had to stop struggling to keep from adding more pain to her arms. She tipped her head back, violet eyes sparkling purple with rage. An answering fire smoldered in his.

"Let me go!" she muttered thickly, breathing heavily.

"With pleasure," Rolt snarled, and abruptly released her without any steadying hand to help her gain footing on the wet floor. He ripped a large, beach-size towel from the rack. "Here." He wrapped it around her, unconcerned by the rough way he handled her, his hands nearly bruising her tender flesh as he tucked the ends of the towel above her breasts. The towel's wide width tickled the back of her legs. "Your virtue and modesty are still intact."

Ridiculous patches of bubble bath dotted his shirt. His clothes were wet where her dripping body had been pressed against him. Beads of water glistened on his muscular arms, clinging to the dark hairs. With a last, insolently raking glance, he turned on his heel to leave.

Alanna, embarrassed and humiliated and enraged

by what he had done, couldn't let him leave with the
last word. It wasn't enough that he was leaving. She
wanted to have the last word, too.

"And don't you ever come near me again!" Her
foot stamped the wet floor in a childish display of
temper.

Rolt stopped in the doorway, motionless for an instant. Then, like the gradual release of a thickly coiled
spring, he turned, seeming more like the giant she
had often likened him to as he loomed before her.
Alanna backed toward the door to her bedroom. The
small space of the bathroom became too confining,
and Rolt followed.

"If I do or don't come near you again, it will be my
decision." His jaw was clenched, biting down on the
anger that vibrated through his voice. "Not because
of any order from you."

"Don't be too sure about that," Alanna said with
bravado as she kept retreating in the face of his sure
advance.

"Really?" he mocked scornfully. "Did you feel
protected last night behind your barricade?"

His indigo gaze flickered contemptuously to the
dresser in front of the hall door. Alanna had been so
intent on not taking her eyes from him that she
hadn't noticed when her retreating footsteps had
brought her on to the carpeted floor of the bedroom.
Had he known it was there last night? Or had he seen
it for the first time just now?

The question must have flashed in her eyes.

"The living room is just below," Rolt reminded her cuttingly. "I heard you pushing furniture around last night and I doubted that you were simply rearranging it at that hour."

"Then you knew!" she breathed.

"Of course I knew," he snapped. "But you don't honestly think it would have stopped me if I wanted to get in this room!"

"I would have clawed your eyes out if you'd succeeded," she warned.

"I doubt that." He laughed harshly in his throat.

Too incensed to realize what she was doing, Alanna tossed her head defiantly. "You try it some time."

"That is an invitation I accept."

The spring uncoiled with a swiftness that caught Alanna off guard. Rolt was before her and she struck at him. He dodged the blow and let it land harmlessly on his shoulder.

His hands grabbed her upper arms, bruising her soft flesh.

She struggled, kicking at him, hurting her bare toes against the hardness of his shins. Flailing and pushing at his chest and ribcage, she tried to prevent him from drawing her against him.

Although failing in that she did succeed in wedging an arm above his, loosening his grip, forcing him to circle her back to hold her. It left her arms free to beat at him, as she writhed and twisted in his iron embrace.

The blows she rained on his chest and shoulders

didn't faze him so she aimed a fist at his mouth, the mocking curl of his lips. She felt it split, the bright red of blood showing against the bared white of his teeth. She had the sense to feel fear at what she had done.

Her eyes widened as he lifted her bodily off her feet and tossed her angrily backward. The bed broke her fall, and a gasp of surprise came from her throat. She stared at Rolt's glowering face, unable to move as he towered above the bed.

Recovering her wits, she started to roll to the opposite side of the bed away from him. But he was too quick for her, grabbing an arm and spinning her onto her back, pinning her to the mattress with his weight.

Her hands strained against him, trying to push him off, but Rolt caught them and stretched them above her head. She stared at him, knowing she was trapped. Her violet eyes were wild with despair as they met the hard glitter of his. He lowered his blood-stained mouth, covering hers in a long, fiery kiss, parting her lips until the taste of his blood was on her tongue.

Her head moved in faint negation, trying to fight yet feeling the will to resist weaken. The heat of his body warmed her skin. The dampness of his clothes added to the heady, masculine scent. The firm touch of his hand on her bare shoulder furthered the destruction of her defenses. The physical ache for fulfillment was real and undeniable, adding to the overwhelming vulnerability that threatened her.

Somewhere Alanna found the ounce of reserve needed to keep her from responding with the fervor she felt. She musn't surrender to Rolt, not after what he'd done to her and Kurt, and used her father to trap her in a marriage she despised. When she felt that last measure draining under his savage passion, she was sure she was lost. As the tiny light of resistance flickered and died, Rolt lifted his head.

With an expression of angry disgust, he moved away from her, standing beside the bed. Her trembling hand clutched the loosened folds of her towel, uncertain whether his release was permanent or temporary.

"This is the way it's going to be, is it?" he said grimly. "A battle of wills? We'll see who gives in first."

With an abrupt turn, he walked away from the bed toward the barricaded door to the hall. Alanna stared, feeling a sudden overpowering need to have his arms around her and the warmth of his body next to hers.

"Rolt," she called weakly after him.

He halted, turning at an angle. "What is it, Alanna?" His voice was curt and unyielding.

A bitterness rose in her throat. For the second time, she had nearly let physical attraction override her self-respect and pride. She hated Rolt.

"Go to hell!" she breathed with sobbing fury.

The line of his mouth curved in a cold smile. "Only with you, my wife." He easily pushed the dresser to its proper position, then walked back to unlock and open the door. There he paused, slicing another look in her direction. "It won't be necessary to erect your little barricade every night. I wouldn't want your attractive figure to become muscle-bound."

As the door closed behind him, Alanna pressed the knuckles of her fist against her mouth and rolled onto her side. The bedcovers were damp where they had lain on top of them. She was filled with the humiliating truth of whose will was stronger. She would have surrendered just now if Rolt had persisted another few seconds. She mustn't let herself fall in love with him, she thought desperately.

Fall in love with him! The phrase was a lightning bolt that jolted her upright. That was ridiculous! How could she even consider such a possibility? Just because funny things happened inside her whenever Rolt came near or touched her, it didn't mean she was falling in love with him, did it? But doubt crept in.

Quickly Alanna reminded herself of the unscrupulous methods Rolt had used to trap her into this marriage. She couldn't possibly love a man who would so coldly ignore his brother's feelings. She mustn't, she insisted with wild frenzy.

The aroma of frying bacon greeted her when she finally came down the stairs. The plague of doubts and fears had been pushed to the back of her mind. Yet, as she entered the kitchen, she eyed Rolt warily, half afraid he would guess the crazy ambivalence of her feelings toward him and take advantage of it.

He was standing in front of the stove, his back to her, tall and broad-shouldered, lean-hipped and muscled. Alanna's skin tingled with the remembering feeling of being molded against his hard frame. She trembled, not wanting to be aware of him. She wanted to flee the room, and would have if Rolt hadn't chosen that moment to glance over his shoulder.

"How do you like your eggs?" There was absolutely nothing in his expression to indicate that the tumultous scene in her room had ever taken place.

"Over easy." Alanna tried to match his composure.

He cracked two eggs over the skillet and dropped the contents in the sizzling butter in the pan, discarding the shells. "Breakfast is about ready. There's orange juice in the refrigerator. The glasses are already on the table."

Taking the pitcher of juice from the refrigerator, Alanna set it on the small breakfast table in the kitchen. The place settings were already there for two people. She had expected a cold war to exist between them. If not that, then she had thought Rolt would regard her with barbed looks and mocking gibes.

But not this. He was almost companionable—aloof, yes, but still companionable. It made him more dangerous to her hastily reconstructed defenses than before.

THE HONEYMOON WEEKEND passed in that same vaguely congenial atmosphere. They swam, boated, lazed in the sun, and walked in the woods. Rolt's invitations were always accompanied by a silent "You're welcome to come if you like or stay if you don't." They didn't talk much or laugh. They were two strangers doing things together simply because there was no one else to do them with.

Yet Alanna found herself identifying days by the times Rolt had touched her. When they had gone boating, he had lifted her from the dock to the boat, and out again on their return. Swimming, he had helped her up the ladder. Walking through the woods, he had occasionally held her hand to steady her over rough ground. The times he had smoothed suntan lotion on her shoulders and back were the hardest to forget. The contact had never lasted long, but Alanna was disturbingly conscious of his touch

At any time, she knew that the slightest indication from her would have changed the impersonal contact to a caress. The knowledge pulsed below the surface each time they were together.

Early Monday morning, she was awakened by a knock on her door. Blinking the sleep from her eyes, she sat up, hugging the covers about her.

"Yes?" she said thickly.

The door opened and Rolt stood outside. He was impeccably dressed in a suit of a pale tan check, and Alanna thought fleetingly of how well he wore the garb of civilization. Fathomless indigo eyes examined the sleep-tossed curls of her tawny hair and the hazy vulnerability of her expression.

"I'm on my way to the office," Rolt told her impassively. "I'll be home around eleven-thirty for lunch. It will be expected that the first few weeks I lunch with you whenever it's possible."

"Of course," she nodded.

"I'll see you then," he said shortly, and left. A few minutes later she heard the sound of the car pulling out of the drive.

Three times during that week he came home for lunch. Twice Alanna went into town to visit her parents, mentioning Rolt's name as often as she thought a new bride should. The weekend was almost a repeat of the first, with the exception that on Saturday night they were invited to a dinner with a business associate and friend of Rolt's. It wasn't difficult to pretend to be the adoring wife, especially when Rolt was acting out the complementing role.

It seemed to Alanna, as she smoothed suntan lotion on her legs, that admitting that she could fall in love with Rolt made it more likely that she would. She fought against the prospect, constantly reminding herself what a despicable character he was. But it was difficult to keep summoning the old hatreds when he offered no new fuel to keep the fire burning. If he had forced himself on her, taken her against her will, she would have had fresh cause to detest him.

As it was—she sighed and poured more lotion into her palm. As it was, it was becoming impossible to live under the same roof with a man as virile and compelling as Rolt and remain immune. It wasn't natural for a man and a woman to live together and separately. This falsely platonic relationship couldn't last. She had seen the look in his eyes sometimes when he watched her. He wanted her—that hadn't changed.

Initially her goal had been to make Rolt's life miserable. Now she was concentrating all her efforts on not being caught in her own trap. Her chances of succeeding were growing dismally smaller each day, and she felt frustrated and helpless.

Staring out over the landscape of Minnesota green, she tried to lose her thoughts in the beautiful view from the sundeck. She smoothed the lotion on her shoulders, stretching her arm to try to reach more of her back.

"I'll do that."

Alanna jumped at the sound of Rolt's voice. Her rounded eyes saw him standing behind the screened sliding door leading into the dining room. His suit jacket was off and hanging by the hook of his finger behind him.

She glanced quickly at her wristwatch lying on the table beside her lounge chair.

"I didn't expect you for another hour," she murmured self-consciously. "You did say one o'clock?"

He slid the screen open and stepped on to the planked sundeck. "I got away earlier than I thought," he shrugged, and tossed his jacket over the back of a lawn chair, continuing his path to her.

Alanna set the bottle of lotion down, flustered by his early arrival. "I haven't even started lunch, I—" She started to rise, but the hand on her shoulders pushed her back down.

"It doesn't matter. I'm not particularly hungry...for lunch." There was an infinitesmal pause before he added the last word that had Alanna's heart skipping beats.

Her lashes fluttered down in silent acceptance of the hunger of her senses for his touch. The lounge chair creaked once in protest when his weight settled in the cushion behind her. The coolness of the suntan lotion was on her back, then firmly smoothed over her skin.

Not an inch of her back was ignored. His hands followed the curve of her spine to the small of her back, stroking the sensitive skin with disturbing results. Manipulating fingers moved over her waist and ribcage, tantilizingly near the swelling of her breasts, then traveled on to the nape of her neck.

A fire was being kindled inside her, the warmth was building. She knew it would burst into flame at any moment. She moved her shoulders in an instinctive and unwilling signal of protest.

"That should be good enough," she said with a faint breathy catch to her voice.

Rolt didn't stop. "It's more effective against sunburn if it's rubbed in." The husky tone was nearly as seductive as his hands.

"Don't!" Alanna tried to conceal her uneven breathing. She slid forward on the chair's cushion to elude his hands.

With one she was successful, but the other hand curved around the front of her shoulder and half turned her to face him. She had difficulty meeting his gaze, so she looked at the opened front of his shirt, an equally evocative sight. His hand moved to the side of her neck, a thumb raising her chin. His eyes smoldered with the same desire that burned inside her.

"It's still no, is it?" Rolt questioned grimly.

"Yes," Alanna whispered, "it is."

She knew the pulse in her neck was hammering against his fingers, but she couldn't make her heart slow its rapid beat. Her lips had parted slightly, unconsciously inviting. His gaze slipped to them. For a taut second, she wished Rolt would ignore her answer, but it wasn't to be fulfiled as he released her and stood up, the bronze mask of control covering his features.

"I guess you'd better fix lunch so I can get back to the office," he said blandly.

CHAPTER EIGHT

"I'M AFRAID YOUR SWITCH is burned out," the mechanic said.

Alanna looked at him blankly. When it came to the inner workings of a car, she knew absolutely nothing about it. The only time she thought about it was when the car wouldn't run, as was the case now. "Can you fix it?" she asked anxiously.

"Yeah, I can fix it all right," the man nodded, "but not tonight. I don't have a replacement for your particular model of car on hand. And there isn't time to make it over to the parts store before it closes. I could have it ready for you first thing tomorrow morning."

Alanna sighed and handed the mechanic the keys. "Go ahead and tow it into your shop and fix it. I'll be by in the morning to pick it up."

"Between nine-thirty and ten o'clock, it should be ready," he agreed, and walked away.

"Daddy—" she turned to her father standing in the driveway with her "—can I borrow your car to get home? I'll bring it back in the morning when I pick mine up."

Dorian Powell shook his head regretfully. "I'm

sorry, honey, but I have a meeting tonight or I'd be glad to lend it to you. I'll give you a ride home, though."

"Oh, no, dad, I can't let you drive all that way." Alanna felt like a heel refusing him, but she knew what an acceptance of the offer would lead to before she reached home. Her father would suggest that her mother accompany them, just for the drive. Once they arrived, she would be obligated to invite them to see her husband's house. They had been hinting at such an invitation for over a week now. There simply wasn't any way Alanna could explain the separate bedrooms without destroying the image of a happily married couple. "You could drive me to the plant and I can ride home with Rolt. He'll be finished work soon."

Her father's disappointment was obvious, but he couldn't argue with the practical suggestion. "I'll let your mother know where I'm going and be right out."

"Tell her goodbye again for me," Alanna said, since her first attempt to leave her parents' home had been postponed when the car had refused to start.

Later, during the drive to the taconite plant, her father commented, "Rolt is really making a success out of this operation. You can be very proud of him, Alanna."

"I am," she smiled briefly.

"Before your wedding, he hinted that there might be an increase in my stock earnings. It turned out to be quite a substantial one," he informed her. "He's quite a businessman, Rolt is."

"Yes, he's very clever." Silently Alanna realized that he had kept his word about helping her father.

She also noted that the lines of strain and tension had disappeared from around her father's mouth and eyes. The burden must have been heavy for its removal to make such a difference.

When they stopped at the entrance gate, the security guard smiled broadly in recognition. "Good afternoon, Mrs. Matthews, Mr. Powell." And they were waved on through.

Her father dropped her off at the door near where the black Mark V was parked, insisted that he couldn't come in with her if he wanted time for a leisurely meal before his meeting, and left.

Many of the office staff recognized Alanna when she entered the building. She hadn't been to Rolt's office since that night he had coerced her into marrying him. The curious glances and occasional smiles of greeting from the staff made her wonder if they were remembering the numerous times she had dated Kurt before suddenly marrying Rolt. She felt uncomfortable and defensive.

Rolt was in the outer office talking to a man in a dark suit when she walked in. The disturbing warmth of his gaze melted away the chill of apprehension that had hurried her through the halls. She moved eagerly toward him, ignoring the upturned face of his secretary.

"You wouldn't believe what's happened," Alanna smiled.

She would have stopped in front of him, but his arm encircled her waist and drew her against him to receive his kiss. Her lips automatically responded, bringing a dark glow to his eyes that she found difficult to sustain when he raised his head.

Turning to the bemused man watching their greeting, Rolt said, "My wife, Alanna. Tom Brooks, with the shipping firm out of Duluth."

There was a self-conscious flood of color to her cheeks, brought on more by her unrestrained response than by the fact that it had been witnessed.

The man smiled briefly at Rolt. "I had heard you had left the folds of bachelorhood. I was hoping this was your new bride you were kissing." He turned to Alanna. "It's a pleasure to meet you, Mrs. Matthews."

"Thank you." She shook his hand, Rolt's arm slackening its hold around her waist only slightly.

"Now what brought you here?" Rolt prompted. "You said something had happened." For a blank instant, Alanna met his gaze. "Have you forgotten?" he chided mockingly.

"No," she breathed a shaky laugh. "My car broke down—something to do with a switch of some sort. It won't be fixed until the morning so I'm here to cadge a lift home."

"I think that can be arranged." Then he frowned, a brow arching. "How did you get here?"

"Daddy brought me. I stopped by to see them to-day and the car wouldn't start when I went out to go home," she explained.

"I have a to go over a few things with Tom first." He glanced at his secretary over the top of Alanna's head. "There is nothing else after that, is there, Mrs. Blake?"

"No, sir."

"As soon as Tom and I are finished, we can leave," Rolt said.

"I promise I won't keep him long, Mrs. Matthews", the man smiled.

Alanna glanced around the room, the vague feelings of discomfort returning at the thought of waiting in the office until Rolt was free to leave. She didn't want to be the recipient of any more speculating looks from the staff. Sitting in the office would be like being on display.

"I think I'll wait in the car, if that's all right," she told Rolt.

"Of course." He removed his arm from around her waist and reached into his pocket. "It's locked. You'll need the keys."

Taking them, Alanna smiled politely at the other man. "It was nice meeting you, Mr. Brooks." With a quick, faintly uncertain smile at Rolt, she walked from the room into the hall.

As she moved down the corridor, a familiar figure approached from the opposite direction. It was Kurt, but the ready smile was in absence and the easy charm wasn't sparkling in his eyes. He seemed so much different from the man she had once loved that he seemed a stranger.

Alanna's steps faltered as she realized she had referred to her love in the past tense. She hadn't seen Kurt since that night he had found her with Rolt. Suddenly he seemed the answer to her problem. If she could talk to him and explain what had happened, maybe she would be able to rekindle her feelings for him and thus provide herself with an immunity to the emotions Rolt was arousing in her.

"Hello, Kurt," she greeted him quietly when he was nearly level with her.

He nodded briskly without speaking, his expression masked, his shoulders stiff. He would have walked on by, but Alanna stopped, partially blocking his path.

"Please don't walk away," she begged.

He halted, his abrupt manner indicating he was anxious to be on his way and didn't welcome her interruption.

"I can't think of anything we have to say to each other," Kurt responded coldly.

"There's a great deal to say if you would only listen," Alanna argued pleadingly, keeping her voice low. "You never gave me a chance to explain my side of what happened."

"I don't see what there is to explain. It's all fairly obvious." His gaze was as bleak as an arctic sky.

"Things aren't the way they appear on the surface."

"Aren't they?" he mocked. "You did marry my brother."

"Do you know why?" Alanna gazed at him, silently pleading for him to give her the benefit of doubt. "The real reason?"

"Alanna," he sighed in irritation, "what would be the point? What would it change?"

"I hope it would change the way you think of me," she answered honestly. "It hurts to have you thinking I'm some kind of tramp."

Kurt turned his head away, staring at the blank corridor wall. "Okay, so you want to talk, explain whatever it is. Go ahead, I'm listening."

"Not here." Alanna glanced around, conscious of the people in the offices along the hall. "It's too public. Besides, Rolt will be coming shortly."

"You want to meet me somewhere, is that it?" he inquired with a faintly mocking smile.

"To talk, yes," Alanna qualified. "I'll meet you for lunch tomorrow at twelve-thirty."

Alanna didn't want to be seen with Kurt at a public restaurant. The word of her meeting would spread too quickly back to Rolt.

"Could we meet at the Iron Range Interpretative Center?" she asked.

"You don't want Rolt finding out, is that it?"

"Yes," she admitted.

He shook his head as if questioning the wisdom of what he was agreeing to. "I'll meet you there tomorrow." Without another word, he walked past her.

THE SKY WAS OVERCAST, a gloomy pearl gray with darker, threatening clouds on the horizon. The whispering wind carried the warning of an approaching storm, chilling the temperature.

Alanna buried her hands deeper in the pockets of her yellow windbreaker and watched Kurt's car drive into the Center's parking lot. Behind her was the striking concrete and glass building of the Iron Range Interpretative Center.

The site, atop the crest of the old Glenn Iron Mine, held a commanding view of the inactive, open-pit mine with its man-made gorges and canyons. Nature trails wound around the base of the modern building.

When Kurt got out of his car and walked to meet her, Alanna turned to stare at the impressive structure.'

It didn't seem to matter that her marriage to Rolt was not one born out of love. The sting of guilt was still there to make her feel uncomfortable about meeting Kurt.

She chided herself for being so rigidly moralistic. She was nervous, though, when Kurt stopped beside her.

"It's beautiful, isn't it?" Her angle of view provided a glimpse of the bridge jutting out over the mine. "Have you been inside?"

"No."

"Neither have I recently. Not all the exhibits were there when I went through it. It's complete now, though, I understand. But what I saw was fascinating." Remembering the flag exhibit in a mirrored room, Alanna thought about the people who had immigrated to Minnesota from all over the world. "It doesn't deal with just the discovery of iron and its mining and development. It tells you about the people, too, their life, working the mines, in the summer and in the logging camps in the winter." She was talking rapidly, avoiding the issue that had brought them here.

"The people were mainly immigrants from Rumania, Yugoslavia, Germany, Norway, Sweden, England, Ireland, and many other countries. It was a melting pot of cultures, religions and languages. There's a film that tells some of the reasons why they came to America and their first impressions. Most of them couldn't speak English and were unaccustomed to the extremes of the Minnesota climate. Homesick—"

"Alanna," Kurt broke in impatiently, "it's all very interesting, I'm sure, but that isn't why I'm here."

"I know." She sighed reluctantly, turning to face him, then lowering her chin to stare at the ground. "I don't know where to begin."

"Try at the beginning," he suggested dryly. "Why did you marry Rolt if it wasn't for love or money?"

"Because I hated him." Again the usage of past tense gave her a momentary qualm. Before Kurt could make a remark, she hurried on. "I know Rolt gave you the impression that I'd been seeing him while I was going with you, but it wasn't true. He came over to the house once on a Sunday afternoon and that was the only time I saw him except when I was with you." There was disbelief in his gaze and it made Alanna impatient. "I was with you practically every night. I didn't have time to meet Rolt—unless you think I slipped out to meet him after you'd brought me home."

"All right." Kurt conceded the possibility she was telling the truth. "If you hadn't been seeing him, why did you go to his office that night?"

"Because he said he knew something about my parents."

"Your parents?" Her answer startled him.

Alanna breathed in deeply and began to explain about the financial problems her father had incurred, concluding with, "Rolt said he would help dad without him ever learning about it *if* I would marry him."

A spatter of raindrops fell. Kurt took hold of her arm. "We're going to get wet standing out here. Let's go to my car." With shoulders hunched against the scatter of fat drops, Alanna hurried toward Kurt's car. Neither spoke as Kurt opened the passenger door for her and walked around to the driver's side. Rain pattered on the roof, the only sound for several seconds once they were inside.

"How do you explain that love scene I walked in on?" Kurt asked finally, sliding her a challenging look. "You weren't by any stretch of the imagination resisting him."

"No, I wasn't." Alanna stared at the twisting hands in her lap. "I haven't any excuse for that, except that your brother is very experienced at physically arousing a woman. It was an excercise to prove I wouldn't find his lovemaking unpleasant."

"Obviously you don't," Kurt muttered thickly, gazing straight ahead.

"I—I don't know." She shook her head, feeling the piercing swiftness of his gaze turning to her.

"Come on, now, Alanna," he growled beneath his breath. "You've surely had enough time to make up your mind by now."

She hesitated, pressing her lips together.

"There was a wedding, Kurt, but it isn't really a marriage."

"What are you trying to say?" He looked at her skeptically.

"We have separate rooms," Alanna murmured, lifting her chin with a trace of defiance as she flushed self-consciously.

"Rolt? My brother? He agreed to this?" Kurt frowned incredulously.

"He's waiting for me to come to him." She hooked a curl behind her ear.

"So far you haven't," he said, yet managing to put a question mark at the end.

"How could I—" The rest of the sentence remained in her throat. It should have finished with "—when I love you," but Alanna couldn't get the words out.

Her gaze desperately sought Kurt's face, trying to find the attraction she had once felt. Now it was the faint resemblance to Rolt that stirred her senses. She looked quickly away, blinking at the tears burning her eyes.

Kurt's hand touched her shoulder, gripping it gently to turn her toward him. He leaned forward, his mouth descending on hers. The burning ardor of his kiss ignited only a gentle flame of emotion, not the powerful passion that Rolt's kisses sparked. Her lashes remained lowered when Kurt set her away, hiding her disappointment and wishing she hadn't kept this meeting with Kurt. It wasn't fair of her to hurt him more.

"It isn't there, is it?" he said quietly. "What we once had," he added.

Alanna shook her head, keeping her chin lowered, as she acknowledged that he was right. She heard the regret in his voice and shared it.

"To be honest, Alanna," Kurt continued quietly, "that last week I thought something was missing. I had the feeling you were withdrawing from me each time I held you in my arms. That's why I was so ready to believe that you had been seeing Rolt on the side. It was easier somehow to think of losing you to him than just losing you because you didn't love me. It doesn't make sense, I know, but—that's the way I felt."

"I'm sorry, Kurt," she murmured. "I wanted to love you. I really thought I did."

And it would have made it so much easier to protect herself from falling in love with Rolt. Seeing Kurt had opened her eyes to the truth. She already was in love with Rolt.

"We've both had quite a few things cleared up today. We understand ourselves and each other better." He sighed as if he wasn't certain that was good.

"No hard feelings, Kurt?" She tipped her head to one side, her gaze sad and wistful.

"No." He smiled grimly. "I'm still sorry I lost you, but I'm not bitter any more. Eventually the hurt will leave, too."

There wasn't much left to say, and both of them knew it. Alanna reached for the door handle and released the latch. She smiled weakly over her shoulder at Kurt.

"Take care," she said in goodbye.

"You, too." But there was a tightness in his expression that said he still loved her, regardless of her change of feelings.

By the time Alanna had driven back to the house by the lake, the intermittent rain had stopped, but the sky remained threatening. The meeting with Kurt had left her feeling dispirited and restless, confused by a problem she didn't know how to solve. Loving Rolt should have made things simpler; instead they seemed complicated.

She wandered through the house, listening to the thunder rolling closer. Lightning flashed in crackling arcs and tongues. Dinner was in the oven when the

wind came, whipping and bending the conical tops of
the pines. The rain came with a rush, blinding sheets
hammering at the windows. The fury of the storm
grew steadily.

The table was set and dinner was warming in the
oven, but Rolt wasn't home. At first Alanna didn't let
herself become concerned. The storm had probably
held him up. The roads would be slick and the visibil-
ity poor.

When one hour stretched into two hours late, panic
set in. Alanna dialed the number of his private line at
the office, but there was no answer. She called the
entrance gate, only to have the security guard on duty
tell her that Rolt had left the plant almost two hours
ago. She began imagining problems as trivial as a flat
tire and soon progressed into accidents with Rolt lying
injured in some ditch along the way.

When she picked up the telephone the third time to
call the police, the line was dead, knocked out by the
storm. Raking her fingers through her tawny hair,
Alanna glanced at the rain-coated windows. A jab of
lightning exploded somewhere close by and thunder
shook the glass.

The front door burst open, and Alanna pivoted.
Her first thought was that the howling wind had
blown it open. A rush of moist, turbulent air swept
into the living room, cooling her cheeks. A molten-
silver flash of lightning illuminated the night, lingering for several seconds.

Outlined in the doorway was the dark silhouette of

a man. Dark hair was wind-tossed in rumpled waves. His stance, feet slightly apart, was intimidating. Rain glistened on the wooden planks outside the threshold. In that charged and lightning brilliant instant, the man didn't seem real—a mythical being, a giant.

The giant moved, and the breath that had been caught in Alanna's throat was released in a joyous sigh. She raced to the doorway as Rolt stepped in, dripping rain, his expensive suit plastered against his muscular frame. His sun-bronzed features gleamed wetly, lashes dark and spiky from the water.

"Rolt! Where have you been?" She ran into his arms.

Her relief at seeing him safe and apparently un- harmed was too great to be held in. She buried her face in the wet lapel of his jacket as he pushed the door closed, shutting out the wind-whipped rain. She could hear the solid, steady beat of his heart.

"What took you so long?" she breathed.

"There was a tree across the road, and I had to walk," Rolt answered, his breath warm against her hair although his voice was oddly aloof.

Alanna became aware of the way she was clinging to him. The wetness of his clothes was beginning to be absorbed by hers. Her hands slid from his shoulders to the hardness of his chest as she levered herself away. Thunder rumbled threateningly and she shivered at the violence of the storm he had walked through.

"Afraid of storms?" Indigo eyes watched her.

"Not usually," she laughed nervously. "But I was worried about you. I called the plant and the guard said you'd left two hours ago."

"Yes, I did. I'm sorry you were worried."

"Yes, well, it couldn't be helped." His hands were resting lightly on her hips. Alanna edged a few more inches from his chest, nerves jumping, "Dinner is ruined, I'm afraid, but it's probably just as well. As soaked as you are, the best thing would be some hot soup. And a dry change of clothes."

When she would have moved away, his hands tightened on her hips. "Were you really worried, Alanna?" The hard brilliance of his eyes searched her face.

"Of course I was." A finely strung tension gripped her. She felt suddenly defensive. "I'm not some unfeeling monster, Rolt."

"But you think *I* am," he said in a quiet accusation.

Alanna looked away. "I don't." Her pulse was quickening under his disturbing regard. "I mean, not really, just sometimes." She was stammering, faltering over words and explanations. "There are times when you are ruthless—you have to admit that."

"It seems to be the only way that works."

The bronze mask was molded in uncompromising lines.

"This isn't the time to be discussing it." Alanna pushed more firmly against his chest. "If you'll let me go, I'll fix your soup." She tried to sound firm and not affected by his touch. "And while it's heating, you can go upstairs and get out of those wet clothes before you catch pneumonia. A hot bath wouldn't do any harm. I'll bring the soup up and you can have it in bed," she said, trying to treat him as a child in need of motherly attention.

"No." It was short and clipped, his fingers biting into her bones. A muscle leaped in his jaw. "I'm not going to bed alone, Alanna, not any more."

The gasp of surprise had barely begun when he fluidly swept her off her feet into the cradle of his arms, checking the sound. He held her there, staring enigmatically into her startled face. His drenched clothes chilled her skin, but Alanna didn't notice it. The fire burning inside distracted all her thoughts.

Slowly he walked to the stairs, carrying her effortlessly in his arms as he mounted the steps. At the head of the stairs, he turned to the master bedroom. The drumbeat of her heart sounded louder than the thunder and more primitive in its origins.

THE TELEPHONE RANG. Alanna slowly opened her eyes, not sure of the sound, awareness creeping slowly through her sleep-drugged body. Sunlight flooded the room with blinding force. She was lying on her side, the coolness of a sheet against her naked skin. A furnace warmth burned her back, extending over her waist and stomach. Her hand slid down to investigate the heat and encountered the curling hairs of an arm.

She stiffened for an instant, then languidly relaxed under its pressing weight. Rolt's warm breath caressed her shoulder in even breathing, stirring the tangle of hair at the base of her neck. She snuggled closer to him in heady contentment.

A delicious thrill ran through her veins at the memory of his easy mastery of her responses. She hadn't known that pain could mingle so easily with rapture, nor that there could be such a joy in physical union.

A flush colored her cheeks as she remembered the way their unsatiable hunger had turned them to each other a second time in the night. She savored the memory. A smile curved her mouth. At last she understood her mother's 'heavenly plateaux.' She had glimpsed them last night in Rolt's arms.

The discordant ring of the telephone harshly interrupted her reverie. With a start, she realized it was the sound that had wakened her initially. Fortunately she was lying on the side of the king-sized bed nearest the telephone on the night stand.

As she started to move to answer it, the arm around her waist tightened instinctively. She glanced quickly at Rolt over her shoulder. He was still sleeping. The rough angles and planes of his face were gently strong in repose.

Not wanting to disturb him, she stretched an arm toward the phone. Her fingertips gripped the receiver and lifted it off the hook before it could ring again. Absently, she realized the line downed by the storm must have been repaired.

"Matthews residence." She spoke softly into the mouthpiece, her voice still slightly thick with sleep.

"Alanna, this is Kurt," came the reply. "Did I wake you?"

"Not exactly." She was suddenly and embarrassingly conscious of Rolt lying beside her. It flamed her cheeks.

"I've been trying to call for over an hour, but the storm knocked your phone out last night."

"Yes, I know," she murmured.

"I was calling to find out if you know what time Rolt left for the plant this morning. I was supposed to meet him at nine and he isn't here yet," Kurt said.

Her gaze slid to the clock on the bedstand. It was a quarter past ten. She swallowed, unable to tell Kurt that Rolt was still sleeping, with her.

"No. No, I don't know. He might have overslept." Alanna allowed a portion of the truth to slip out.

"There were quite a few trees downed by the storm. He might be waiting somewhere for a road to be cleared," Kurt suggested.

"Yes. If I hear from him before he sees you, Kurt, I'll have him call," she promised quietly.

"Thanks, I—"

Alanna never heard the rest of Kurt's sentence. A coolness bathed her stomach and waist as Rolt's arm moved. His fingers firmly took the telephone receiver from her hand. Breathing in sharply, she turned partially on her back to meet the wicked light in the dancing dark blue of eyes. His weight shifted so that he was pressing her shoulders on to the mattress.

"Kurt, this is Rolt." Even as he spoke into the tele-

phone, his mouth was exploring the corner of her
eyes, the curve of her cheek and jaw, mortifying
Alanna beyond words. Kurt must have been as
stunned as she was, "Are you there, Kurt?" Rolt inquired with faint mockery, the line of his mouth curving against her skin.

Teasingly he traced the outline of her lips. They
parted tremulously under the tantilizing caress.
Alanna moved weakly in protest, embarrassed that
Rolt should be making love to her while talking to
Kurt and that she should be letting him. Rolt's weight
wouldn't release her. She twisted her face into the
pillow and he shifted his attention to the vulnerable
curve of her throat.

Distantly she heard the hollow sound of Kurt's
voice coming through the wires, but she was too
swamped by the dizzying sensations to hear his words
above her quickened breathing. Gooseflesh shivered
deliciously over her skin as Rolt found a particularly
sensitive spot on her neck.

"Sorry about breaking our appointment. It was
quite late before we got any sleep last night and
Alanna was trying to be the considerate wife by letting
me sleep in this morning. Weren't you, darling?"
Rolt laughed softly against her throat, sending more
shivers of irrational pleasure dancing down her spine.

"Rolt, don't," she whispered achingly.

"Let's change it to one-thirty. Will that work out
for you?" The fiery trail of his mouth continued its
downward exploration, investigating the shadowy

hollow between her breasts, then choosing the rounded curve of one for closer inspection. An uncontrollable shudder of desire quaked through her, and her fingers culed into the muscled bronze of his naked shoulders. "And you'd better tell Mrs. Blake I'll be unavoidably detained until noon."

He lifted his head and leaned across Alanna to replace the telephone receiver on its cradle. When he moved back, his arms were on either side of her head, propping him above her. He lazily studied her flushed cheeks and the feverish violet of her eyes.

"Now where were we?" he murmured.

Much later, Alanna lay in the crook of his arm, her head resting against the solidness of his chest, rising and falling at last in even breathing. The dreamy afterglow of satisfaction softly curved her mouth. If she didn't move for a thousand years, it would still be too soon.

But the emptiness of her stomach was reminding her that she hadn't eaten since noon yesterday and she doubted that Rolt had either. Reluctantly she moved away from the warmth of his body, and slipped out of bed. Aware of the sunlight shining brightly on her naked curves and Rolt's eyes watching her, she walked self-consciously to the masculine robe lying over the back of a chair and put it on, tying a knot in the sash at the waist.

"Where are you going?" Rolt asked in a lazy, caressing voice.

"To fix breakfast." Alanna turned, brushing the

hair away from one side of her face with a nervous hand.

He was propped on his side, an elbow beneath him, the bedcovers down around his waist. His bare chest and shoulders gleamed bronze in the sunlight, contrasted by the white of the sheets and pillows. The dark light in his disturbing gaze made her blood run swiftly.

"Come here."

Alanna walked to within a few inches of the bed and stood. His hand caught at the ends of the sash and drew her forward until her knee was bent on the mattress. Her senses threatened to whirl her into abandonment again.

"You didn't have dinner last night. You must be hungry," she murmured in semi-protest.

"My appetite doesn't seem to be for food." He released one of the ends of the sash and pulled at the other to loosen the knot, watching the front of the robe open. "I think I'll burn all your clothes and make you wear only this," he said idly, then glanced at her reddened face, "except that I'd probably never leave the house."

His gaze held hers for heart-stopping seconds. The hungry rumbling of her stomach snapped the invisible thread that bound them. Rolt smiled suddenly.

"You'd better fix that breakfast. I don't want you fainting on me."

Alanna was at the bottom of the stairs before her legs finally stopped trembling. When Rolt came down, he had showered and shaved, and was dressed in a business suit. The smile he gave her when she set their plates on the table contracted her heart. The difference was so great when his mouth curved without the jeer of mockery. The silence during the meal was golden and wonderful.

Rolt finished his third cup of coffee and glanced at her. "It's time I left."

Alanna nodded, rising from her chair. "I'll drive you to where you left your car."

They walked to the front door. There, Rolt halted and faced her. Alanna stopped, glancing uncertainly at him, meeting his probing look.

"Will you move your things into my room?" His hand slipped inside her robe, cupping her breast. "Or shall I move my clothes into yours?" he asked quietly.

"I'll move mine," Alanna promised with faint breathlessness.

His exploring hand slid around her to the small of her back, drawing her against him to receive his hungry kiss. The clean scent of him was a heady fragrance. His mouth carried the taste of rich coffee. It remained on her lips when he lifted his head.

"We'd better leave now or I'll never go," he declared huskily.

The door was jerked open and Alanna walked through it, hiding a pleased smile. It was a wondrous discovery to learn that she could shatter his composure, that his control wasn't as iron-clad as she had believed. He was as vulnerable to the ardor of her kiss as she was to his. The rain-washed world outside looked beautiful and bright. Her heart sang joyously.

CHAPTER NINE

THE silver gleamed against the white linen tablecloth. The crystal goblets sparkled with rainbow brilliance. The high polish of the china plates glistened richly. Alanna moved the floral arrangement an inch, wondering if Rolt would notice that they were the same flowers that had been in her wedding bouquet. She stepped back and surveyed the table. Candles stood tall and straight in their silver holders; a bottle of champagne was chilling in its bucket of ice.

In the kitchen, the soup was warming on a burner. The salad was waiting in the refrigerator with the dessert. The steaks were marinating, ready to be put under the broiler. Everything was in readiness for Rolt's arrival.

Including herself. Alanna had been floating on a cloud all day. And tonight she wore a lavender cloud, a filmy dress of chiffon with a plunging neckline. It made her feel ethereal and feminine and excitingly alluring. Gliding at least an inch or two above the floor, she moved to the sliding glass door near the sundeck and frowned impatiently at the western sun.

"Oh, please go down early tonight," Alanna requested urgently. "We can't have a romantic candle-light dinner with you shining in."

A car stopped in front of the house. She pivoted toward the wide hall connecting the dining room to the living room, and waited breathlessly in anticipation. The front door opened.

"Alanna?" Rolt's voice demanded an answer.

"I—I'm in here." A bubble of happiness nearly cut off her voice. She didn't rush to meet him. She wanted him to come into the dining room and see her preparations for their evening.

Long strides quickly brought him into view, and the smile of welcome froze on her lips at the coldness of his expression. His gaze swept over the table, stopping icily on her.

"What's this?" A victory celebration?" he accused.

Alanna shook her head in disbelief. This couldn't be the same man who had left the house this morning, or more accurately this noon.

"I don't know what you're talking about," she answered uncertainly.

"Don't you?" Rolt jeered. Alanna winced, until now thinking she had seen the last of his harsh mockery. "Kurt didn't keep his appointment this afternoon."

She looked at him blankly. "I don't understand."

"Really?" he retorted with contemptuous disregard for her confused expression. "He left a message with my secretary saying he was unavoidably detained. That was his exact phrase—unavoidably detained." His repetition of it reminded Alanna that Rolt had used the same expression this morning. The implication jolted her. "It was a perfect twist of the knife by my brother, don't you think?"

"What are you saying?" Alanna breathed incredulously.

"What's the matter?" His lip curled sardonically. "Didn't you know that my little brother had already let the secret out? Were you hoping to let it slip tonight?"

"You don't know what your talking about!"

"Don't I?" Rolt pivoted sideways as if he couldn't stand to look at her. Just as abruptly, he glared at her. "You had me fooled completely. I never dreamed for an instant that you would leave me this morning and meet Kurt this afternoon. And you knew it, too."

"I didn't meet Kurt," Alanna protested.

A dark brow arched arrogantly over indigo scorn of his gaze. "Where were you this afternoon, Alanna? I phone here and there wasn't any answer. You weeren't at your parents' either."

"I went into town—" she gestured wildly toward the bottle of champagne "—to buy the champagne for our dinner tonight."

"By sheer coincidence, it happened to be that you were gone at the same time Kurt was unavoidably detained, is that right?" A muscle leaped savagely in his jaw.

"It happens to be the truth. I went into town,

bought the champagne and came straight back, without meeting anybody!" Her eyes burned with bitter tears.

"Do you expect me to believe that?"

She sunk her teeth into her lip for a painful second. "I don't expect anything!"

Her voice was choked. She knew she couldn't endure his cutting sarcasm without dissolving into tears. She started to hurry from the room, but Rolt intercepted her, grabbing her arm and spinning her around.

"Do you deny that this isn't the first time you've met Kurt since we've been married?" he snarled.

She blanched. Her eyes widened in alarm. The line of his mouth became ominously grim at her reaction.

"You thought I didn't know about your meeting with Kurt yesterday, didn't you?" He pulled her against his chest, coldly looking into her stunned face.

Yesterday—it seemed much longer ago than yesterday that she had met Kurt in the parking lot of the Iron Range Interpretative Center. If Rolt knew about that, then it was no wonder he thought she had been with Kurt today. But after last night and this morning, how could he think that?

"H—how did you find out?" she faltered.

"Office gossip. It has a way of traveling fast, especially if it has the potential of scandal. Someone overheard you arranging to meet Kurt when you talked to him in the hall," he explained with cutting disdain.

"I met him, yes," she admitted, "but it wasn't a

sordid thing, not like you're trying to make it sound."

"You mean he didn't hold you in his arms or kiss you?" Rolt mocked. "Not even for old times' sake?"

It didn't matter what she said, Rolt was going to believe the worst. Alanna gritted her teeth against the pain tearing at her heart.

"I am not going to discuss it with you," she declared tightly. "What's the use of defending myself when you've already tried and convicted me?"

"The facts speak for themselves," he retaliated.

"Facts! What do you know about facts?" Emotion strangled her accusing voice. "You wouldn't know a fact if it hit you in the face!"

"I know one fact." Rolt let go of her arm and stepped back, his jawline white with the savage ferocity of his anger. Alanna had the impression that he had released her and put distance between them to keep from throttling her. "You aren't going to see Kurt again."

If he had phrased it in a less dictatorial way, Alanna would have admitted that she wasn't interested in Kurt, but his command was a red cape waving in front of her.

"Do you think you're going to stop me? How? By locking me in? Posting guards like a prison? I'd find a way to escape just to spite you, if nothing else. Nobody tells me what to do! I don't take orders from anybody!" She flared in full temper. "I will see who I want to, where I want to and when I want to—and you won't stop me!"

"You swore once that you'd make my life miserable. At the time, I thought it was amusing, but I underestimated you." The quietness of his voice was more menacing than if he had shouted in rage. "You're more cunning and deceitful that I realized. You are my wife, Alanna. You try to see Kurt again and you'll discover the consequences of trying to get back at me."

"What consequences could be worse than what's already happened to me?" Tears glistened in her eyes from pain and anger. "I don't have a monopoly on making life miserable. You took out the first patent on it, destroying my relationship with Kurt and blackmailing me into marrying you! As for being your wife, that's a circumstance that can be changed. And I will change it, Rolt. Nothing can make me stay married to you."

"Nothing?" he responded smoothly. "What about your mother and father? The day you file for a divorce my support of them is finished."

"My father will have to pay for his own mistakes the way I'm paying for mine," Alanna answered without hesitation. "And marrying you was the biggest mistake of my life."

"I'll fight you, Alanna," Rolt warned. "You're not going to divorce me and marry my brother."

"I won't marry Kurt." There was a brief, negative movement of her head. "I don't want anything to do with men. None of your sex is worth the pain you cause. There's something very ironic in this situation." Her mouth curved bitterly. "When Kurt falsely accused me of having an affair with you, I blamed you for manipulating things to get what you wanted. Now you're accusing me of seeing Kurt, an accusation just as false as his was. This time, there's no one to blame but me, because I didn't know anything about men. But you taught me, Rolt. You taught me well."

She started to walk past him, intent on leaving, but he stepped into her path. Her shimmering gaze lifted coolly to his face, surprised by the look of a wounded animal in intense pain that she saw in his dark blue eyes.

Immediately his gaze hardened into blue steel.

"Where do you think you're going?" he challenged.

For an instant, Alanna thought she had seen, in the tormenting ache in his eyes, the same excruciating pain that she was feeling. But she realized it was damaged ego, disgusting male pride, too fragile to withstand any rejection.

"I told you, I'm leaving," she stated forcefully. "Leaving this house. Leaving this marriage. Leaving you."

"What do you want me to do?" His jaw worked convulsively. "Do you want me to get down on my knees and beg you to stay? Crawl to you? Is that what you're seeking? Do you want me to grovel at your feet so your triumph can be complete?"

"That would be a sight to see, the giant of Mesabi

at my feet." Alanna laughed bitterly through her tears.

"Does it give you satisfaction to know that you can bring me to my knees?" Rolt demanded harshly.

"None at all." Not when it was pride causing his downfall.

"Nothing I can say or do will make any difference, is that it?"

"There is one thing I'd like to know." Her chin quivered, but pride kept her gaze level. "Before that seduction scene last night, did you know that I'd seen Kurt yesterday afternoon?"

"Yes."

Even though she had braced herself for the affirmative answer, Alanna still couldn't stop herself from recoiling as if struck by his hard, unapologetic voice.

A hot tear burned down her cheek.

"What a fool I made of myself!" she breathed achingly. "You made love to me because you were afraid Kurt would steal my virginity before you did. I never realized love could be such a humiliating emotion."

"Love!" Rolt grabbed her shoulders and shook her violently. "You don't know anything about love!" Pulling her on her tiptoes, he drew her within inches of his face. "Do you know what it was like all those weeks when I sat in this house knowing you were out on a date with Kurt, imagining you in his arms, kissing him? Have you any idea how it felt to see that dislike in your eyes every time you looked at me?

Love." He groaned the word huskily, anguish-darkened eyes sweeping over her face. Alanna was stunned, certain her ears were deceiving her.

"The first time I saw Dorian Powell's teenaged daughter I was fascinated by her. When you matured into a woman, I couldn't stop myself from loving you. I still can't. Yes, I forced you to marry me—I tricked, I blackmailed, I manipulated. I think I would have done anything to have you as my wife. Okay, so I didn't play fair, but whoever said life was fair? I thought I could make you love me in time. Last night—" He shook his head and let her go, not finishing the sentence. "And today you met Kurt."

From somewhere Alanna found her voice. "But I didn't meet Kurt."

"Alanna, don't lie to me," he sighed heavily.

"I'm not lying. Are you?" she whispered.

Rolt frowned, confused. "Lying about what?"

"Do you—love me?"

She had to pause to swallow the lump of apprehension in her throat.

"Isn't that what I've been saying all along?" Pain furrowed his brow. "I love you, Alanna."

The statement was not accompanied by any flowery speeches or declarations, yet its stark simplicity carried more depth of emotion than the others could have done.

"I love you, Rolt." At his pained glance of skepticism, Alanna hastened to elaborate. "I've been fighting against falling in love with you since our wedding, trying to make myself believe it was only physical attraction, but I wasn't very convincing. The only reason I met Kurt yesterday was because I wanted to reassure myself that I still loved him. I'm not sure if I ever did love him. I only know that I don't love him. He's nice and I'm fond of him, but it's you I love."

His gaze narrowed, thoughtful and wary. "Today—"

"Today I went into town, bought champagne and came straight home." Alanna repeated her earlier explanation. "I didn't see Kurt, I was too anxious to come back to fix our dinner this evening. It was to be the first real dinner we'd shared as husband and wife, a second wedding night with candlelight, champagne and flowers. Because I love you."

She was caught in the crush of his arms, his face buried in the dark amber curls of her hair. Her hands instinctively slid around him. Alanna felt him shudder.

"It's enough if you only think you love me," he muttered thickly. "Just give me a chance to make up for all the things I've done. Just don't leave me, Alanna. Don't leave me."

"I'll never leave you," she whispered the vow.

Rolt cupped her face in his hands, his compelling gaze holding the brilliance of hers.

"Never is a long time," he reminded her with faint wryness.

"Never," Alanna repeated the promise.

The muffled cry of a loon echoed over still lake

waters. The sun smiled and winked at the empty place settings on the dining room table. He knew he could take his time about sinking below the horizon. It would be a long time before anyone thought about lighting the candles.

my VALENTINE 1992

Celebrate the most romantic day of the year with
MY VALENTINE 1992—a sexy new collection of four
romantic stories written by our famous Temptation
authors:

GINA WILKINS
KRISTINE ROLOFSON
JOANN ROSS
VICKI LEWIS THOMPSON

My Valentine 1992—an exquisite escape into a romantic
and sensuous world.

 Harlequin Books ®

VAL-92-R

HARLEQUIN Temptation

Rebels & Rogues

All men are not created equal. Some are rough around the edges. Tough-minded but tenderhearted. Incredibly sexy. The tempting fulfillment of every woman's fantasy.

When it's time to fight for what they believe in, to win that special woman, our Rebels and Rogues are heroes at heart.

Matt: A hard man to forget . . . and an even harder man not to love.

THE HOOD by *Carin Rafferty*.
Temptation #381, February 1992.

Cameron: He came on a mission from light-years away . . . then a flesh-and-blood female changed everything.

THE OUTSIDER by *Barbara Delinsky*.
Temptation #385, March 1992.

At Temptation, 1992 is the Year of Rebels and Rogues. Look for twelve exciting stories, one each month, about bold and courageous men.

Don't miss upcoming books by your favorite authors, including Candace Schuler, JoAnn Ross and Janice Kaiser.

RR-2

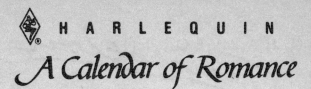

♦ H A R L E Q U I N

A Calendar of Romance

Be a part of American Romance's year-long celebration of love and the holidays of 1992. Experience all the passion of falling in love during the excitement of each month's holiday. Some of your favorite authors will help you celebrate those special times of the year, like the romance of Valentine's Day, the magic of St. Patrick's Day, the joy of Easter.

Celebrate the romance of Valentine's Day with

**#425 VALENTINE
HEARTS AND
FLOWERS
by Muriel Jensen**

Read all the books in *A Calendar of Romance*, coming to you one each month, all year, from Harlequin American Romance. COR2